I0639801

COVERT: JAYDEN

EAGLE TACTICAL BOOK FOUR

WILLOW FOX

SLOWBURN
PUBLISHING

Covert: Jayden

Eagle Tactical Book Four

Willow Fox

Published by Slow Burn Publishing

© 2021

Cover by Slow Burn Publishing

Image(s) used under license from Shutterstock.com.

All rights reserved.

No part of this book may be reproduced or transmitted in any form or by any means, electronic or mechanical, including photocopying, recording, or by any information storage and retrieval system, without permission in writing from the publisher.

CHAPTER ONE

Skylar

The music blared over the speakers, making it difficult to hear myself think. Not that there was much to think about.

I downed a shot of tequila and then another.

"Bad day?" the bartender asked.

His first name was Jayden. I didn't get his last name, and I'd been coming to the bar a lot.

Mostly, to figure things out, which really meant hide from my brother and his girlfriend.

Jayden also wasn't a bad view to enjoy after work, imagining our bodies tangled together, hot and sweaty.

Too bad I didn't have the courage to invite him home. Then again, I didn't exactly have a home of my own.

The truth was that imagining him naked and the two of us wrapped up in the sheets was a welcome relief to my boring and inconsequential life.

"Something like that," I said under my breath.

While it wasn't a great day, working at the coffee shop was the only job I had been qualified for.

Besides, no one seemed to be hiring. Plus, I needed to save my money for a place of my own instead of blowing it on overpriced liquor, but it was easier to come here and stare at the hottie of a bartender.

There was something about him.

Dark and mysterious.

Tattoos covered his arms, which peeked out from under his black t-shirt. "Are those real?" I asked and gestured to the ink on his forearms.

I needed more friends.

My brother had a slew of tattoos, but I was unmarked and a blank slate. I couldn't tear my gaze away from Jayden's forearms.

"No, I spend every morning doodling with a permanent marker on my skin to impress the ladies," Jayden said.

Snarky.

I downed my shot and gestured for him to pour me another one.

He grabbed the bottle of tequila and poured the amber liquid into a shot glass. "You know, Skylar, you could just ask me out if you want to see me. You don't have to come to the bar every night after your shift."

My arms rested on the bar, and I leaned my head into my arms, face planted.

An uncomfortable groan spilled out past my lips.

"What's that?" Jayden asked, laughing under his breath. "Did I embarrass you?" He didn't sound the least bit apologetic.

I'd bet he flirted with all the female customers— anything for a bigger tip.

It probably worked too.

He was good-looking, albeit with a dark and mysterious vibe, and that look he shot me made my knees weak.

He was every bit a bad boy.

I didn't have to glance up to know he had a wide, smug grin across his face. With a heavy sigh, I lifted my head and stared up at him.

"Are you guys hiring?" I needed a job that paid enough so I could rent a place or buy something, eventually.

All my money went to car repairs, insurance, and liquor. Maybe I was staying out too much.

"Not the bar..." his voice trailed off.

That caught my attention. "But you know someplace that is?"

He reached for the empty shot glass and took it away, not refilling it with another drink. "Jayden?"

He glanced around before he leaned closer.

What was he worried about?

There were a few patrons in the bar, but it was loud and difficult to hear anything over the pulse-pounding music.

"Come with me out back." Jayden gestured to another one of the staff members that he was going for a break.

I followed Jayden through the darkened hallway and then out the rear exit of the bar.

The loud music seemed distant from behind the closed door. My ears rang.

"You know some place that's hiring?" I asked again, my voice louder than I intended.

His answer was a whisper, his voice quiet, his tone making it clear that we needed to be quiet about it. "I need a partner for an off-the-books type of job. It pays in cash."

I liked cash, especially if I could avoid claiming it with the government.

"What's the gig?" I asked. "I'm not going to be a drug mule." I'd seen enough movies to know that never ended well for the mule.

Besides, I had no intention of spending any time behind bars.

Jayden snorted under his breath. "Drugs aren't involved, but it's not any less dangerous."

"Okay." I could handle danger.

He stared at me with sharp eyes. He glanced me over from head to toe, twice. "You can't tell anyone about the job."

I pretended to lock my lips like I did as a kid. "Don't worry. It's not like I have friends around here."

"That includes your brother and his girlfriend," Jayden said.

I shifted the weight on my feet. "You know my brother?" That made me a bit uncomfortable.

What else did he know about me that I wasn't aware of?

He gave a silent nod. "You live with him."

"How the hell do you know that?" I pointed at his chest and poked him in the process.

He didn't so much as flinch. "Your driver's license has his address."

Oh. He was right. I had changed my identification after I moved into town. "You know my brother." It was more of a statement than anything else.

How did the two of them know one another? I'd never seen them converse, and Jaxson never mentioned Jayden.

Jayden didn't elaborate further. "Can you keep a secret from him or not?"

"He doesn't know I come here after work every day," I said. That was a secret I kept from him. There were a dozen or so more.

"I'm serious, Skylar. If you work for me, no one can know. It'll be a deep undercover operation."

He sounded just like Jaxson when it came to his Eagle Tactical business. "Please, don't tell me you work for my brother." I wasn't sure I could handle that news.

"No, and I can't tell you who I work for, so do me a favor and don't ask," Jayden said.

"Okay."

He must have been C.I.A. or some other agency. As long as I got paid on time, I could look the other way.

"What's the job?" I asked. "What do you need me to do?"

"Marry me," Jayden said.

I coughed, shocked by his proposition. "Excuse me? That's crazy."

He couldn't be serious. I wasn't marrying him for money or any other reason.

"Relax. It's part of the assignment. I need you to post pictures of our engagement on your social media accounts," Jayden said. "I'll get you a ring. We'll make it look official. We need to get my boss' attention. He already doesn't trust me, and I need him to show an interest in you."

Okay, so maybe he wasn't C.I.A., and his boss was a bit shadier. Did he work for the mafia or a drug kingpin?

"You want your boss to hit on me because he thinks I'm engaged to you? What kind of bosshole is he?" I asked.

That was a terrible idea.

Jayden laughed under his breath and exhaled a heavy sigh. His eyes looked tired, with dark circles underneath. "I can't tell you anything more. Are you in or not?"

"Will I be risking my life?" I asked.

I had a feeling that whoever his boss was, it wasn't some top-notch guy.

He stalled for a moment before answering. Was he deciding whether to answer me honestly or not?

"Yes. I'll pay you a thousand a week."

If I was risking my life, I wanted more money. "I want double."

"Done," Jayden said a little too quickly.

Maybe I should have tripled it.

"Swing by my place tomorrow after you quit your job at the café. Say around ten o'clock in the morning. Give me your phone, and I'll put my address in it."

He tapped away at my phone screen, inputting his contact information before he handed me back my phone. "Remember, you can't tell anyone about this arrangement."

"I swear I won't."

Who would believe me, anyhow?

CHAPTER TWO

Jayden

I hadn't wanted to involve Skylar. Hell, I hadn't wanted to involve anyone else in my mess, but I needed a man on the inside. Or rather, in this case, a woman.

Could I trust the spunky little sister of my military brother? Jaxson and I had barely spoken to one another.

Well, that wasn't entirely true. He'd offered me a job with his team at Eagle Tactical.

I'd had no choice but to refuse.

Jaxson was completely unaware of my connection with Enzo Ricci. On occasion, I also worked alongside Sheriff Nelson and the tri-county task force, but even they didn't know my connection with Don Ricci.

Bringing Skylar into the job was against every protocol, but I needed her help.

My work went deeper than just bringing down the off-gridders. Nearly every last one of them was dead, except for Emma. She was now in prison, awaiting sentencing after pleading guilty.

Maybe I should have thanked the mafia for slaughtering my enemy, the one I had to live with, sleep beside, and pretend to be one of, to gather their trust and intelligence.

It wasn't Don Ricci who had murdered the off-gridders. As the saying goes, the enemy of my enemy…

A firm knock resounded against the wooden door.

"Just a sec," I shouted and grabbed my Glock. I wasn't taking a chance, ever. I glanced through the peephole to see the five-foot-two beauty on the opposite side.

My hormones raged at one glance at her. Her shirt was cut with a low V, dipping into her cleavage, leaving little to the imagination.

Down, boy.

She was here for a job, not to fuck me.

That was too bad.

I unlocked the door and made sure she was alone.

I let her inside my apartment, and I shoved my Glock into the waistband of my pants.

The apartment was dark. I left the window shades closed to make sure no one could see inside.

Was I paranoid?

Yes, but for a good reason.

Skylar folded her arms across her chest. Her long locks fell across her face.

The longer I stared at her, the more irritated she looked.

"So, what's the job?" she asked.

I stalked across the room to a dresser drawer, yanked open the top handle, and pulled the drawer hard. I dug in between my socks and retrieved the tiny jewelry box. I tossed it at Skylar.

She fumbled with the box, nearly dropping the black velvet before flipping open the lid. "You were engaged?"

"Just something I keep around," I answered. That was all she was getting in the way of an explanation. "We need to spend the afternoon together, taking lots of pictures, making it look somewhat believable that we're happily engaged."

Skylar's brow furrowed. "Somewhat believable? You don't think I can do my part and act madly in love with you?"

I merely shrugged. "I haven't seen your acting skills. Besides, it's not me you have to convince."

She leaned against the bed and plopped down on the edge. "Are you going to tell me why I'm doing this? I would never have pegged you for the type who has to pay for a girlfriend to take home to your parents."

That's not what this was. Not in the slightest, but I held my tongue. "Don't worry. The entire arrangement is one hundred percent professional."

Skylar pursed her lips and patted the bed beside her. "It doesn't have to be."

Was she testing me? Enzo would expect some level of intimacy if we were seen together, but I didn't plan on that happening.

The truth was my plan was shitty at best. I needed Enzo to trust me, and he'd been offering me girls left and right, women he intended to auction off and sell to the highest bidder.

It disgusted me.

He wouldn't leave it alone, and I had lied to him, told him that I had a fiancée at home. Which meant I needed a girl who would have my back.

Emma was in prison.

There hadn't been anyone else since her, and even then, she had been a means to an end.

Another job. One that had turned complicated.

I don't usually sleep with my protégé, but with Emma, she'd been hot, fierce, and offered herself up to me.

I hadn't been able to say no. She had bewitched me.

"Well?" Skylar asked. "What's the gig? I strut around town showing off my flashy engagement ring?" She slid the diamond band onto her ring finger before she thrust out her cell phone.

I needed her to get close to Enzo. He still didn't trust me, not completely.

"It's more complicated than that. I need you to gather intel for me on Enzo Ricci."

"Excuse me?" Skylar pushed herself off the mattress. "Isn't that the shady billionaire who just moved into town?" Her voice raised an octave as she spoke. "Is he like a drug dealer or something? He kind of looks like he works for the mafia."

Apparently, word traveled fast.

"He's my boss. Already, he believes that I don't trust him. Which I don't. But that's beside the point. I need you to gather as much information from the girls he's holding. I'm looking for a girl named Lexa Clarke."

"Gather information. How, exactly, and who is Lexa Clarke?" Skylar asked.

This wasn't just a risky job. It was a lifestyle and not one that I wanted to commit myself to, but there'd been no other choice.

"You're going to accompany me to a party that Enzo is hosting at his home. He's already panicking because the shipment of girls that was due in was delayed."

"Delayed?"

The girls weren't exactly delayed. I had intercepted the shipment, having gained access to the manifest and released the girls into federal custody. Enzo didn't know it was me who had betrayed him. If he had, I would have already been dead.

I didn't want to worry Skylar or give her any intel that could be used against me later. The less she knew, the better.

"It doesn't matter about the girls. What matters is that you're going to join me at his home as my fiancée."

"I'm not following on how I'll be gathering information on the girls he's holding. Will they be at the party too?" Skylar asked.

"Doubtful. I'm sure he's holding them someplace at the compound on his property. Probably a basement or cellar."

"Let me guess. You want me to sneak around without getting caught?" Skylar asked.

"Yes. Dante will likely be guarding the access point, so you may need to flirt with Enzo's second in command, Dante."

"Second in command? What is he, mafia?"

I didn't answer. I wasn't about to lie to her. But yes, Enzo was the head of the Italian mob who owned most of the west coast and had branched outward. They dealt in smuggling guns, drugs, and girls.

Skylar exhaled a heavy sigh. "Wonderful."

"All you have to do is flirt with him if you get caught. He's a sucker. Easy to manipulate. Don't worry."

"Flirt with him? You're underselling the job." Skylar wasn't an idiot. Maybe I underestimated her.

"He's in over his head right now with the shipment of girls who have gone missing. Dante needs help. If you seem eager to please, he's desperate to keep

Enzo happy. He'll easily betray me to get on Enzo's good side."

CHAPTER THREE

Skylar

I laughed at his ridiculous plan. "Are you insane?" He wanted me to sneak around a heavily guarded mafia fortress and flirt with the mob boss' second in command if I got caught?

"I know you're scared," Jayden said, "but once we get the intel we need from your wire, then we'll pull you out and shut down the entire operation."

It sounded too easy.

"What happens when they see the wire?"

I already knew the answer. They'd kill me.

He rested his hands on my shoulders as he stared at me, towering from above. "No one is going to find the wire. It won't be taped to you like in the movies. Our technology is better than that. I promise you'll be fine. In and out without a hiccup. You won't be at the party for more than a few hours."

A lot could go wrong in a couple of hours.

"Then why did I quit my day job if this is a one-week operation?" I asked.

He didn't answer me.

Exactly.

He knew that this was dangerous and went deeper than just attending a party.

We'd have to keep up the charade after the party too. How long would we pretend to be married?

Maybe Jayden wasn't risking his life, but I'd be putting myself straight into the hands of men who were monsters.

He may have wanted this to be over within the week, but a lot could go wrong.

I still didn't understand his crazy plan. "Why pretend to marry me? Are you really that desperate for a plus one to the party?"

I swallowed the lump that formed in my throat.

Jayden was a handsome guy and the thought of pretending to be married would have been fun if he'd invited me to a wedding or we pretended to be together to make an ex-girlfriend jealous.

This scenario was dangerous and it scared me.

"You'll be fine." His face showed no hint of emotion.

What was Jayden hiding from me?

"What benefit do you get out of us being engaged?" I asked, tilting my head to the side. There was more to it, something that I wasn't seeing.

Jayden laughed under his breath before he answered, "I've been trying to get Enzo to stop throwing women at me."

"Poor Jayden," I mocked. When he didn't so much as flinch at my remark, I leaned closer to him.

He wanted us to pretend to be engaged. Then we needed to pretend to like one another.

Maybe we needed to practice kissing too?

I was fully on board with making out with him. He was attractive and had a nice physique. It was clear that he worked out regularly.

I rested a hand on his chest and let it slide down to his belt buckle. "Who is Lexa Clarke? Is she your girlfriend?" I wanted to know who the girl was who needed saving.

Jayden cleared his throat. "What are you doing?"

"Shouldn't we know everything about one another? I mean, what happens if I get caught the minute we're inside Enzo's home and someone asks me about a birthmark or tattoo on your body?" My fingers unclasped his belt buckle.

He had a lot of tattoos on his arms. Where else did he have tattoos?

"That isn't going to happen," Jayden said, his voice rough and deep. He raised an eyebrow at me.

"And how do you know that?" I hadn't let go of him yet. "You're throwing me into danger. The least you can do is make sure that I'm fully prepared."

His lips descended hard and fast on mine, surprising me.

With one hand on his belt buckle, my other hand traveled up into his hair, pulling him closer and tighter against my body.

Everything inside of me ached with need.

I'd never felt this desperate before.

A moan spilled out past my lips as we kissed and he yanked me harder, closer, tighter.

There was a roughness to him that I'd never experienced.

I longed for more. I liked it a lot.

Jayden pulled back. "Fuck," he muttered and took another step away from me like I'd burned him.

He was hot and cold.

What the hell was going on with him?

"Who is Lexa Clarke?" I asked again, this time louder and with more insistence.

Is that why he stopped anything further from happening between us?

Was he in love with another woman?

I waited for Jayden to elaborate on why he wanted me to sneak around his boss' complex.

The heat and fire that he had beyond his gaze turned dark.

"She is my niece."

The weight of his words hit me like a ton of bricks. That was the last answer that I had expected.

"What?" I said, unsure I heard him correctly.

"Lexa is my niece. About eighteen months ago, I received a call that my brother and his family were in a horrible car accident. He'd taken the family off-roading on a camping trip, and their SUV had gone over the edge of a cliff. Lexa was the only survivor. According to the police report, she had been outside of the vehicle and had directed her father around the sharp turn when the tire hit a soft spot and slipped off the ledge of the road."

"Oh my gosh." I lifted my hand to my lips and covered my mouth for a brief moment.

Jayden ran a hand through his hair. "If that wasn't horrible enough, she never made it to Breckenridge.

The police considered her a runaway as did DCFS. I did some investigating on my own, though, and tracked her whereabouts to a human trafficking ring that operated just outside of where she'd gone missing."

I slumped back onto the mattress. "That's terrible." That poor girl had lost her family and then was held against her will, with men probably doing horrible things to her.

Jayden's expression remained grim. "It is. She's just a child, barely fifteen. I haven't been able to track her any further than Enzo Ricci. Every trail leads directly to him. Hell, for all I know, she's already been bought and sold, but I can't give up. I won't give up. I refuse to leave her behind."

His eyes were glassy, his pupils dark, like two saucers. He exhaled a heavy breath as he paced the length of the apartment.

His place was small for someone who could afford to pay me two grand a week in cash. It was clear he was trying to keep a low profile. Working at the bar was probably a side gig to keep suspicions down.

"What do you need me to do?" I asked.

CHAPTER FOUR

ARIELLA

"Morning, Freckles." Jaxson pulled me tight against his body beneath the covers.

"Is it time to get up already?" I mumbled through heavy-lidded eyes.

Any minute, Izzie would come tearing through the bedroom door. If we were lucky, she wouldn't climb onto the mattress and start jumping on the bed.

She'd been a terror lately, and while I had thought I missed those years, boy, was I wrong.

Jaxson's warm breath caressed my skin as he kissed a soft trail of butterfly kisses against my neck and down my cleavage, dipping his head beneath the blankets.

I moaned, shifting on the bed to get comfortable but also knowing this was a bad idea. "Jaxson," I whispered, my voice raspy and filled with need.

"Shhh, we have to keep it down," he said, reminding me that we could get interrupted.

Buried beneath the covers, his lips made a warm path down my stomach and across my navel.

He didn't linger, going right for his intended target. He slid my panties down and trailed a slow path of warm kisses up my inner thigh to his intended destination.

I grew restless from his teasing and bit down on my bottom lip to keep from moaning as the bedroom door flew open.

Oh crap.

"Jaxson," I moaned, trying to tell him that his daughter was about to come barreling into the room.

His name was the only word that I'd been able to get out.

"Ariella!" Izzie squealed as she ran into our bedroom.

His tongue stopped working its magic, and I whimpered in protest.

Focus.

I needed to pay attention to his daughter and also scold Jaxson later for not having a lock on the bedroom door.

"Where's Daddy?"

Jaxson climbed out from beneath the covers, revealing himself to his daughter.

"Daddy!" Izzie climbed up onto the mattress without so much as an invitation. "What were you doing under there?"

His sly grin didn't help settle my heart. He made me breathless. My heart pounded wildly in my chest as I tried to calm down.

"Trying to sleep. Ariella makes all sorts of noises when she sleeps," Jaxson said.

"I do not!" I smacked his arm playfully. "You are full of lies."

Izzie glanced between us, her eyes narrow and sharp. She was the spitting image of her dad.

"Daddy doesn't lie," Izzie said and stood on the bed.

"Of course, she's going to side with you," I said, gesturing at Jaxson.

Jaxson grabbed Izzie by the waist and tackled her to the bed with tickles.

"Daddy!"

I laughed under my breath.

It was no wonder she loved running into the bedroom and jumping on the bed.

She always stole her daddy's attention.

"You're not a monkey." Jaxson reminded her. "No jumping on the bed."

Izzie thrashed and giggled before Jaxson let up. "Okay," she said with a loud sigh. She sounded just like her father.

I slid out of bed. My nightgown covered the fact my panties were buried somewhere beneath the bedsheets. I'd have to find them later.

"Any plans for this afternoon?" Jaxson asked, glancing at me as I headed toward the bathroom to brush my teeth.

"Harper invited me to take her shopping for maternity clothes and baby stuff. I think Hazel will be joining us too."

It was Sunday, which meant no work, and I was looking forward to unwinding with a girls' day.

Already, it was much needed with the added stress of knowing that my sister was planning on visiting.

I hadn't seen Delphine in months. She finally booked a flight and decided to come crash with Jaxson and me for a week at our place.

She'd insisted on coming to meet the man I was living with and wanted to make sure he wasn't anything like Ben.

"Also, Delphine is coming into town tonight. I'll have to pick her up at the airport around dinner."

"So, you want me to cook?" he said, teasing me.

Jaxson plopped himself at the edge of the bed while I brushed my teeth.

"Last night at the cookout, Hazel showed me her phone."

"Yeah?" I wasn't sure where he was going with his comment.

Izzie sat on his lap and traced her fingers over the tattoos that marked his skin. She seemed bored but was keeping herself entertained for the moment.

I began brushing my teeth and stepped out of the bathroom to listen to Jaxson.

"Skylar's engaged."

I nearly spit the toothpaste out of my mouth. I coughed and hurried back to the sink to spit.

"Are you sure?" I asked. Skylar hadn't so much as brought a boyfriend home since she moved in with her older brother.

"She posted it all over her social media account. I can't believe she didn't tell us!" Jaxson lifted Izzie into his arms and stood.

He headed toward the bathroom. Jaxson's footsteps were heavy against the floorboards as he paced the length of the room.

I finished brushing my teeth before stepping back into the room, leaning on the doorframe."

Obviously, it was a spur of the moment decision. Maybe she was worried about how you'd react?" I said.

Skylar and Jaxson hadn't been particularly close, at least from what I could surmise. There didn't appear to be any bad blood between them, but they weren't best friends, either. It was as if they had nothing in common except their parents.

"What's engaged?" Izzie asked. She wiggled in Jaxson's arms, wanting to be put down.

He planted her feet on the ground, and Izzie tore out of the room.

With a heavy sigh, he followed after his daughter, probably to discover what trouble she found her way into next.

I hadn't known Skylar that well. Even though she lived with us, I barely saw her. The glimpses that I'd gotten, she reminded me so much of Izzie with her carefree, snarky attitude.

Jaxson hurried down the stairs, and I followed a few steps behind, waiting until they were out of the bedroom to retrieve my panties from beneath the blankets.

A few minutes later, I joined the two of them in the kitchen. Jaxson was preparing breakfast while I came over to offer my assistance.

"What can I do to help?" I asked.

"I've got it," Jaxson said with a shrug. "Right now, it feels good to keep busy."

His jaw was tight. His eyes were narrow and filled with determination as he measured each ingredient to put into the plastic bowl. This wasn't about making breakfast. Was it still about Skylar?

"I'm sure she intends to tell you," I said.

Jaxson huffed under his breath. "Doubtful. The post was from well over a week ago."

"Maybe she doesn't know how to tell you? You're her big brother. She could be intimidated," I said as I began putting yesterday's clean dishes away in the cabinet.

He shot me a look. "That's not it. I know my sister, and she's in over her head. She's marrying Jayden!"

"Who is Jayden?" Izzie asked.

"How about I take Izzie with me for a girls' day? We're just going to do a little shopping later this morning. It might give you time to stop by the café where your sister works and find out what's going on? Talk to her."

"Yeah, I'll do that." Jaxson exhaled a loud sigh as he mixed the batter for the pancakes. "Are you sure you're okay with all this baby shopping and planning a baby shower for Harper? Lincoln told me that you offered to throw her a party."

"Harper doesn't have any other friends here," I said, reminding Jaxson that she had upended her life from Los Angeles to live in Breckenridge with Lincoln.

Jaxson and Lincoln were buddies. I was doing this as much for Jaxson as I was for Harper.

I put the last of the dishes away in the cabinet and spun around to face him. "Besides, I like spending time with her."

"What about Hazel? She could do the baby shower. I'm sure if you ask her, she'd be happy to help facilitate things."

Jaxson turned the stove on.

"What is this really about?" I asked. I had a feeling it had little to do with the baby shower but something else.

He glanced at Izzie, stalling.

I doubted she even understood what we were discussing. "I'll be fine. You don't need to worry," I said.

Once the pan was hot, he poured the pancake batter into the skillet. "I'm sure you will, but is it a good idea? You lost a child."

Izzie's face scrunched up and she tugged on my arm. "Where did it go?"

"Where did what go?" I asked, glancing down at Izzie.

"Did you forget where you put it like I did with my stuffed ducky?"

I bent down and gave Izzie a swift hug and kiss on the cheek. I didn't want to elaborate on this conversation with her. She was bright, but far too young to be discussing the death of my son.

"How about we get you dressed while Daddy finishes cooking breakfast?" I asked, steering the conversation away from the topic.

Izzie slipped out of my grasp and tore up the back staircase.

"I'm worried about you," Jaxson said as I followed Izzie to the stairwell.

The last thing I wanted was to have a conversation about my deceased son. It was a memory that I always carried with me but didn't ever want to talk about with anyone. That included Jaxson.

CHAPTER FIVE

Skylar

It was a stupid plan, and I was an idiot for going along with it, but I needed the money. I also wasn't risk avert.

I threw myself into terrible situations all the time, but it usually involved sleazy men and too many drinks.

I wore a short, black sequin dress that Jayden had brought home in my size. I'd been staying over at his place the last few days since our fake engagement.

The dress fit nice and snug and hugged all my curves in just the right way.

How had he known my size?

I just couldn't quite reach the zipper.

I held the dress up around my torso. There were no straps.

"Zip me up in the back," I said as I gestured behind me to the open gown.

Jayden stared at me for a minute, his mouth agape.

I tilted my head to the side, smiling at him as he stared at the dress barely covering my assets.

"Did you hear me?" I asked, my voice softer. I could feel the heat creep into my cheeks. I had to be blushing.

"Wow, yes, hold your hair up," he instructed, grabbing a fistful of my hair and tugging. He pulled my neck to the side.

Jayden leaned closer.

His breath hovered over my exposed neck. A shiver coursed through my body.

Was he going to kiss me?

My gaze glanced up toward him.

Jayden leaned closer and whispered against my ear, "Grab your hair, and I'll zip your dress."

Right, the dress.

I'd already forgotten that was why he had nestled up behind me. I was ready to take the damned thing off and have my way with him on the mattress just a few feet from where we stood.

Why did he have this power over me?

I held up my tresses, keeping them out of the way as Jayden's fingers tugged the zipper slowly upward. His breath teased my skin in the process.

I shut my eyes, reveling in the feeling of being wanted.

Did he want me? Or was it just an act?

He had me believing it was real.

I wasn't the one he needed to convince that we were engaged.

His touch on me disappeared, and I felt an emptiness burn through me.

I spun around on my bare feet, staring up at him. Jayden was dressed sharply, in black slacks with a white button-down dress shirt. It was a far cry from his attire at the bar.

Was Jayden trying to impress Enzo tonight or someone else at the party?

"You clean up nice," I said, finding him irresistible as I glanced him over from head to toe.

"Me?" Jayden quirked a sly grin. "You look stunning." His eyes did another once over on my body, admiring my curves.

I would have felt overdressed if I hadn't seen how handsome Jayden looked. If he was uncomfortable, I couldn't tell.

"Big party?" I asked, surprised by the fancy gown. Why else would he have brought home the fancy dress?

"You might say that," Jayden said. He stalked over to his dresser and retrieved a silver heart locket. "The wire you need to wear."

"Jayden." My voice caught in my throat.

His gaze latched onto mine. "You can do this. I have faith in you."

Nervous didn't even begin to explain the feeling of dread that came over me. "Okay."

———

He kept his arm snug around my hip, introducing me to anyone and everyone at the party. "That's Enzo," Jayden whispered into my ear.

I plastered a smile to my face as one hand held a champagne flute and the other clung to my clutch.

I wasn't ready to sneak off and go in search for his niece or any other girls that Enzo might have detained.

Sipping the champagne, I hoped the bubbles would quell my nerves.

Enzo was a thicker individual than Jayden. Jayden was all muscle. Enzo, I suspected, had one too many jelly donuts. He had a sharp nose and a thick head of obviously dyed jet-black hair.

Enzo headed right for us, a stone-cold look of determination across his face.

Feeling his scrutinizing gaze, made me uncomfortable.

A part of me wanted to flee, to run out the front door before he so much as introduced himself, but I couldn't move. My feet were glued to the floor in my new shiny black stilettos.

"Jayden." Enzo's thick Italian accent permeated the ballroom. His voice bellowed beyond the music that played at the opposite end of the room.

A string quartet brought current melodies to life, vibrant and upbeat, but no one danced. Most of the crowd were men, certainly no younger than Jayden, a few were older with salt and pepper hair, everyone dressed sharply in a suit.

"Enzo." Jayden forced a smile as he clasped the other man's arm in a welcoming greeting. His other hand stayed tight around my waist. "I'd like you to meet my better half, Skylar."

Enzo lifted my hand to his lips and placed a kiss on the back of my hand. "It's lovely to make your acquaintance."

"The pleasure is all mine," I said, forcing a smile.

"I hope you both are enjoying the festivities this evening. I have a special treat for your fiancée this evening," Enzo said.

He retrieved a red ribbon and tied it up in my hair around the curls and elastic that had my hair partially up already.

How peculiar.

There was something about him that I couldn't read.

His expression sent butterflies to my stomach.

I refused to let my gaze wander as Enzo stared at me after securing the ribbon. "That's very kind of you, thank you," I said.

Enzo forced a smile before he took a step back and clapped his hands. "Gentleman," he announced.

The music came to a halt while he spoke. "It is my privilege to introduce you tonight to just a taste of what we have to offer."

The lights dimmed. A door from down the hall opened, and ladies dressed in lingerie wandered out onto the floor.

A dozen ladies, scantily clad, eyes glazed over, stood on display. A spotlight landed on them as they huddled together, clearly uncomfortable.

"Remember, if you'd like to sample the merchandise, it will cost you," Enzo said with a hearty laugh. "No woman tonight is off-market. If you see something you like, she's yours to own, tame, and do with as you see fit."

Glancing around the room, I realized there were no other women at the party other than the women being trafficked by Enzo Ricci—and me.

CHAPTER SIX

Jayden

Skylar clutched my arm. Her fingernails dug into my flesh.

I tried not to wince at the sudden pain. I rested my hand atop hers and glanced at her out of the corner of my eye.

While the plan had been to get her to sneak through the compound and gather information, I hadn't anticipated that Enzo would blatantly display the woman as if it were an auction.

Enzo stood just a few feet away.

A wicked grin crossed his features. He snapped his fingers. The music resumed, and the lights brightened the ballroom.

"I'm in charge, darling. Always have been. Always will be, especially while your fiancé works for me," Enzo said and stepped closer to Skylar.

His eyes raked over her body. His gaze stared at her cleavage and then down to the short skirt of the dress she wore. "Looks good on her, don't you think? I do know a thing about fashion."

"He picked this out for me?" Skylar's eyes widened, and her mouth dropped.

The color drained right out of her face.

"Yes, dear," Enzo said. "I wanted to make you the main attraction for this evening."

Enzo grabbed Skylar by the arm and whisked her across the room toward the other women huddled together, trembling in fright.

This was not what we had planned.

Where had Enzo found a dozen women for the event tonight?

The ladies who had been trafficked and intended for this evening had been intercepted. I'd delivered them straight to the feds.

Skylar glanced over her shoulder at me, silently begging me to save her.

CHAPTER SEVEN

Skylar

"Aren't you a beauty?" A dark-haired gentleman with a square jaw and the grayest eyes I'd ever seen looked at me as if I were standing naked, gawking. "I'll take her," he said and gestured at Enzo with two fingers.

"Excuse me?" I scoffed.

I wasn't here as one of his girls to be paraded around, or worse, as some form of entertainment.

While Jayden had wanted me to keep a low profile as his fiancée, this went beyond what even I was comfortable partaking in.

Enzo grabbed my jaw and yanked my face to meet his dark stare. "She's fiery and vibrant. A woman like this would ordinarily cost you double."

"Get off me!" I pushed away from him, only to feel a set of strong, forceful arms against my shoulders, keeping me in place.

Please, let it be Jayden.

I glanced over my shoulder.

It wasn't Jayden. He was being detained by two guards, with a third in quick pursuit to silence him or take him out. I wasn't sure which.

The music continued at a frenzied pace. The violins dropped quick and sharp notes that matched the pace of my racing heart.

Whatever Jayden shouted, couldn't be heard across the distance.

"She's stubborn, but I'm sure you are quite eager to tame and break her, Angelo," Enzo said, speaking about me as if I were a horse and not a person.

Unable to run, the giant behind me held me in place. He was monstrous with his thick hands and tight grip, towering a foot above me. In another life, he could have been a basketball player.

How had he ended up working for Don Ricci?

Hell, how had I been dragged into this mess for a few lousy dollars?

My life was worth more than a measly two grand.

"I'm not yours to have," I said, fighting the grip of the man who dug his fingers into my shoulders. He could have easily lifted and carried me out of the room. Maybe he would if I didn't settle down soon.

The other girls watched me squirm. None of them offered any help. They didn't try to run.

Did they realize they couldn't get away and it was of no use?

I wasn't willing to give up that easily, but it didn't appear as though Jayden was of any use.

Great.

"She is the starlet of the evening, our main showcase," Enzo reminded. "You can have her on one condition."

Angelo practically drooled at the invitation.

"And what might that be?" Angelo asked. He stepped closer, and I suppressed a shiver as his heavy scent of cologne that wreaked alcohol burned my nostrils.

Bile rose up in my throat. I held my hands in tight fists at my sides, my fingernails digging into my palms, leaving an indentation with the pain I felt. I did it to keep from crying.

Neither of these men deserved to witness the fear and trepidation that burned through me.

No, I wouldn't cower at either one of the bastards who thought I was nothing more than a piece of merchandise.

"I don't want you or your men anywhere near my turf. Our business is done."

Angelo folded his arms across his chest. "Who said anything about stepping on your land? You invited us here tonight; don't forget that, Enzo."

"Sir." A gentleman whom I didn't recognize approached Enzo and tapped him on the shoulder.

Enzo glanced at the other man who was a few inches shorter, but they had the same matching eyes, nose, and jawline and could have easily been brothers. "Yes, Dante?"

Dante. I recognized that name.

Jayden had told me that Dante was Enzo's second in command.

I tried not to feign too much interest in what the two men discussed.

They lowered their voices, and with the crescendo of the live band, it was difficult to hear.

Enzo gave a firm nod before Dante hurried through the crowd of people.

I couldn't quite see where he was going.

Had Jayden managed to fight off the guards? Was he bringing reinforcements?

Enzo cleared his throat. "My apologies for the interruption. As I was saying, our business, as I'm sure you're aware, is expanding, and we don't take kindly to other families betraying us. I have it on good authority that your Capo Sergio stole one of our shipments."

I tried not to act like I knew what the two men were conversing about.

But a stolen shipment?

I could only surmise that Enzo was referring to the women who had been trafficked.

If that was the case, then why had Jayden been removed by the guards and I was at the front and center with Enzo and Angelo?

What the hell was going on?

Angelo cocked an eyebrow. "Are you accusing my men of stealing from the Ricci Family? That's quite an accusation, Enzo."

"But not an accusation without merit. I tried to welcome you as a friend, invite you to do business with my family, but you come to my town and start moving in on my turf. Breckenridge isn't big enough for both of our families," Enzo threatened.

"The hell it isn't." Angelo huffed and shook his head.

Enzo's eyes narrowed, but he didn't speak. Not yet.

"I don't take kindly to threats. It doesn't matter if you're Don Ricci or a fucking capo." Angelo yanked my arm and thrust me out of the grip of Enzo's security giant.

I tried to pull myself from his clutches, but he didn't let go. Maybe without the surrounding guards, I could escape the moment he led me outside.

Was that a real possibility or wishful thinking?

I could take one man.

I was screwed if I had to fight an army.

Angelo's top lip snarled with disgust. "You make threats against me. I'm taking her as a promise to you, Don Ricci. We're not finished, not anywhere close."

"Stay out of Breckenridge," Enzo snapped. "And keep the bitch."

Angelo dragged me outside.

A half-dozen men followed us.

Were they with Angelo or guards for Enzo and escorting us off the property? I couldn't tell the men apart, but neither was there to save me.

Angelo led me toward his black SUV, waiting out front by the entrance of Enzo's mansion.

"Get off me!" I thrust myself away from him, kicking and clawing at him with my fingernails—anything to aid in my escape.

"Enough!" Angelo's voice bellowed as he backhanded me across the face, and his finger caught on my chain. He yanked the necklace off, letting it fall to the ground.

My cheek stung, and I tasted the metallic zing of blood on my lips.

"Get in!" Angelo ordered.

One of the guards who had escorted us outside opened the back door of the SUV.

I didn't budge. I wasn't willfully going to further endanger myself. "No," I said.

I wasn't going to bow down to anyone, mafia boss or otherwise.

This was my chance, my one and possibly the only opportunity to escape.

Angelo had climbed into the front seat of the vehicle and blatantly thought I would follow his orders.

I wasn't like those other girls.

Was I afraid?

Yes, but I would fight before I gave in to his demands.

I slipped past the guard who was a solid six-foot-two and hurried as fast as my feet would take me. I sprinted across the driveway and through the grass in stilettos—no easy task.

I headed for the tree line that led to the forest.

How far would I get before they'd catch me?

Would they stop if I made it home, or would they continue to hunt me down?

Bang!

CHAPTER EIGHT

Jayden

Fuck! That did not go as planned.

Enzo had been on to me, but I wasn't sure for how long.

Did he know that Skylar wasn't my fiancée? He'd made no indication that we weren't really together.

Why had he dragged my ass out of the party?

He hadn't executed me. If he believed I'd betrayed him, he would have murdered me in cold blood. Enzo wasn't a forgiving man.

Something had stopped him, but I wasn't sure as to what.

And Skylar was still inside, locked up amongst mobsters and perverts.

What would happen to her?

Two burly guards dragged me, kicking and screaming, out of Don Ricci's house. Neither had said a word to me about what the hell was going on.

They'd tossed me outside and waited until I got into my car and drove off the property before leaving me alone.

I couldn't leave Skylar with those men alone.

I'd gotten her into this mess. It was all my fault.

I drove away from Enzo's home, only out of force, but I didn't leave.

I pulled off the road at the turn, making sure that I had a good vantage point but that his men couldn't easily spot me.

Security cameras were situated outside the property. I couldn't sneak on without being seen, and while most of his security team was preoccupied with the party, there were still a number of guards keeping watch.

Which meant I needed another plan, one that was less conspicuous.

I could hide outside of the boss' house and wait for Angelo DeLuca to leave. Assuming Skylar was forced to leave with him, I could tail his vehicle as soon as he left.

But what if she was dragged down through the compound and led out another exit that I hadn't been privy to?

Or what if they left along with other vehicles, whether part of DeLuca's team or another guest of the party, and I couldn't determine which vehicle she was trapped inside?

A dozen different scenarios played out in my head. None of them ended well for Skylar.

And I had failed in finding my niece.

What chance did I have of rescuing Skylar?

I undid the top couple of buttons on my shirt. I was suffocating.

My phone buzzed in my pocket. Pulling it out, I glanced down at the text message from Dante.

I know you didn't leave. Meet me at the lookout. Ten minutes.

Was this a set up?

If Enzo wanted me dead, Dante would have taken the shot back at the house.

Why meet at the lookout?

I knew the location. It was where we picked up the shipment of girls. The ones who never made it the last time, which was odd considering the number of ladies forced to attend tonight's event.

Where the hell had they come from?

I glanced at the phone once more, considering my options. If I went, there was a chance that I'd miss Skylar, but if I stayed, who was to say that I'd even see her leaving?

Exhaling an unsteady breath, I texted back that I would be there and shoved my phone into my pocket.

I climbed into my vehicle and headed for the lookout point. It would take me every bit of ten minutes to get to where Dante wanted to meet.

CHAPTER NINE

Skylar

I was desperate to escape.

My stupid heels weren't helping me through the grass. I refused to glance behind me, worried that it might slow me down.

Bang!

A shot rang out and whizzed by my head.

"That was a warning shot," Angelo bellowed. "I don't ever miss."

Was he bluffing? He'd been close as hell to hitting me.

I had momentarily slowed down, tripping over my stupid heels.

That was all it took for his men to force me to the ground and frisk me.

Their hands wandered a little too long and close against my skin, under my skirt.

"Get off me!"

It took two guards, one at each side, to drag me to the black SUV.

"No!" I shouted and thrashed about, trying to break free.

"Do you want me to shoot you?" Angelo asked as he stood beside the car. Just moments ago, he'd been seated inside the front passenger seat.

Had he gotten out to shoot me? Was he a better shot than his men, or did he not trust them to do the job?

I slunk into the backseat.

Angelo held the door open for me. There wasn't much choice in the matter.

The two security goons refused to loosen their grip on me until I was in the vehicle.

Angelo slammed the door shut behind me. He climbed into the front seat and glanced back at me. "Don't try anything stupid."

He flashed his gun in my direction, his hand on the trigger.

"I'm just itching to pull it again."

My mouth felt dry. I pursed my lips but didn't say anything.

What could I say that would make him leave me the hell alone?

CHAPTER TEN

Jayden

Against my better judgment, I agreed to meet Dante.

Arriving at the lookout point, I recognized his vehicle.

I reached for my spare gun under the driver's seat and tucked it into my pants, beneath my jacket.

His driver sat in the car while Dante stepped out. His eyes raked over my body.

"Do you have a weapon?"

I wasn't coming unarmed, that's for sure.

"Do you?" I countered, turning the question on him. No doubt he was packing, and probably more than one gun if I knew any better.

"I didn't come here to shoot you," Dante said. He held up his hands in surrender as he drew nearer to me.

Enzo's men had already tossed me out of the party. I didn't want an ass-kicking to go along with it. "That's close enough." I didn't trust him or anyone who worked for Enzo Ricci.

"Your girl, Skylar, she's being used as a pawn for Enzo. He doesn't trust Angelo DeLuca, and neither do I," Dante said.

Why was he telling me this?

The sun beat down on the open expanse of land. From the overlook, there wasn't much to see but miles of forest down below.

Sweat trickled against my forehead from the oppressive heat of summer.

"You have to help me get her out of there. DeLuca will kill her."

Dante's brow tightened. "She'd be lucky if that's all the bastard did to her. Enzo believes that Angelo's stealing girls, skimming from our operation."

"Fuck." That was news to me.

I'd been responsible for ensuring the pickup went without issue.

Gino, Angelo's second, as well as Capo Sergio, had been my main contacts for DeLuca. Both men I'd had the privilege of dealing with were scumbags, but I hadn't even considered that they might not have delivered us the full shipment.

"You have evidence that DeLuca is keeping part of Enzo's delivery to himself?"

"If the boss had evidence, he'd have started a war with DeLuca. He sent your girl in undercover," Dante said.

Did Skylar have any idea what she was doing?

"No way." I didn't believe it. "You sent her in to get killed!"

What game was Dante playing? I didn't trust him in the slightest.

I'd have sworn, based on the fact they'd practically handed Skylar over to Angelo, that they'd been on to me.

Was I wrong?

Had that been a show for Angelo's sake?

"We need DeLuca to believe that we think you betrayed us. It's the only way we're going to find out who the real rat is, stealing Don Ricci's property." Dante took a step closer to me.

"Is she in on the arrangement?" I asked. "Does she know that she's working as a mole for Don Ricci?"

Dante laughed under his breath and gave a slight shrug. "Doubtful. If she did, she'd have told you, and you'd have inevitably stopped it from happening."

He wasn't wrong. There was no way I would have willingly gone along with the plan. It was suicide.

I grabbed Dante's suit and yanked him closer. "When Angelo suspects Skylar is a mole, he'll kill her. When that happens, I'm coming after you and Enzo."

Dante ignored my threat. "Women can be replaced. Don Ricci's been happy with the work you've done; don't disappoint him over some girl."

I drew my fist back and landed a sharp blow to Dante's cheek.

"Skylar is irreplaceable. You're going to help me get her out."

CHAPTER ELEVEN

JAXSON

I stormed into the bar with my fists clenched at my sides. My feet pounded against the floor. I didn't wait for an invitation as I tore around behind the bar, face-to-face with Jayden.

I grabbed him by the shirt lapels, giving him the opportunity to explain himself before I kicked his ass.

"When were you going to tell me that you've been screwing my sister?"

I hadn't quite meant for it to come out like that, so crude and condescending, but I was pissed.

They were engaged, and he hadn't so much as had the decency to show his face anywhere with my sister.

If I hadn't seen it on Skylar's stupid social media account, I wouldn't have even known she was engaged.

Did she not plan on telling me?

Shit.

Was she pregnant?

"Did you knock up my sister?" At least then he'd be doing the honorable thing, marrying her.

"Whoa!" Jayden shoved me backward, knocking my hands away from his shirt and chest. "I didn't sleep with your sister. Chill out and keep your voice down."

His eyes flinched.

Anyone else wouldn't have seen it, but I'd been in combat with Jayden.

I knew that look anywhere.

What the hell had he gotten involved with? "What did you do?" I asked. I ran a hand through my hair.

"Don't worry about it," Jayden said. He turned his back to me.

Where the hell was Skylar?

I hadn't seen her in days.

Usually, she snuck inside late, well past midnight. I hadn't been thrilled with her behavior, but she wasn't my responsibility. Skylar was an adult. Though, sometimes I thought she could use a little growing up, still.

I couldn't just ignore the fact that they were engaged. "You're marrying my sister. If you didn't knock her up, then you have a lot of explaining to do."

I hadn't even known they'd been dating. Skylar had only been in Breckenridge for a short time.

How long had she known Jayden? Days? Weeks? I doubted that it could have been months.

"I'll come by your office in an hour. We shouldn't leave at the same time," Jayden said.

He'd never been particularly paranoid. "You think someone is watching you?"

"I know it."

———

I drove to the office and waited for Jayden to show up. It was a Sunday, so the guys had off, and I had the place to myself.

I wasn't sure that Jayden would stop by as promised, but the sound of a door slamming outside jarred me back to the present.

Jayden didn't so much as knock as he blew in through the front door. "We don't have long until they realize I shut off my phone and the GPS tracker on my vehicle."

"Who's following you?"

"That's not important," Jayden said. "Skylar's in trouble."

A knot formed in the pit of my stomach. That was not what I was expecting to hear.

I thought we came to the office to discuss the fact he was dating my sister and intended to marry her.

"What do you mean, she's in trouble?" He needed to elaborate. It was just the two of us. No one could overhear us like they could at the bar. "Explain yourself, now!" I snapped. He was testing my patience.

"She's with Angelo DeLuca."

"Who the hell is that?" I asked. "And why the hell is she with him?" I yanked my phone out of my pocket.

Was I supposed to recognize the guy's name, because I didn't?

"You can't call her. She doesn't have her phone on her. She left it at my place."

Jayden exhaled a heavy breath, ran a hand through his hair, and shuffled his feet toward the desk.

He looked nervous as hell as he handed me her cell phone.

"Shit." She wouldn't have gone anywhere without her stupid cell phone. She was tied to that thing like it was another limb. "What do you mean, she's with Angelo DeLuca? Who the hell is he?"

"DeLuca is a rival mob boss of Don Ricci. They've been doing business together, but Enzo believes DeLuca is stealing from him."

"What does any of that have to do with my little sister?" Skylar worked at a café. She had no dealings with the mob.

"Don Ricci sent Skylar in as a mole to find out what's been happening."

"What? Are you crazy? You'd better be joking." I stepped closer, closing the distance between us.

I was ready to pound the shit out of Jayden.

What the hell trouble had he gotten her involved with?

Jayden may not have been the cleanest guy, but it didn't seem right that he'd lead my little sister right into the hands of the enemy.

CHAPTER TWELVE

Jayden

I hadn't wanted to involve Jaxson. He was the biggest pain in my ass in existence. The truth was I hadn't forgiven him for kicking my ass at the Blue-Sky Resort when I'd been with the off-gridders and taking hostages.

I hadn't been on board with the plan, but the off-gridders had planned on going with or without me. At least I could make sure no one ended up dead. Plus, I had to keep Emma out of trouble. Little good that had done.

"Where the hell is my sister?"

"I don't know," I said and threw my arms up into the air. "That's what I'm trying to tell you. Angelo DeLuca has her."

"Tell me everything. Start from the beginning," Jaxson demanded.

I quickly recanted my plan and how Enzo had been one step ahead at the party, making Skylar the main attraction. "All I can surmise is the guy who I hired under me has been secretly working with Don DeLuca. Why else would the shipment details always match exactly?"

"Who's your associate? What's his name?" Jaxson rubbed his forehead. He looked pissed as shit.

Not that I blamed him. I'd royally fucked up.

"Benjamin something. I didn't catch his last name." He hadn't given it, and I wasn't asking.

The color left Jaxson's face. "Do you have his contact information or know how we can reach him?"

He wasn't answering his phone. "He's not responding to calls or texts." Not that I expected him to respond to me. I was on the outs, and it was any wonder they hadn't left me dead in a ditch somewhere.

"How long has Skylar been unaccounted for?" Jaxson asked.

"Seventy-two hours."

CHAPTER THIRTEEN

ARIELLA

Harper waddled through the mall. A hand rested on her very pregnant belly as she tried to keep up with us. "I need to pee again," she said.

Harper headed into the bathroom.

Hazel, Izzie, and I grabbed a seat on a nearby bench.

"Think we bought one of everything yet?" I asked Hazel, holding up the six bags of maternity and baby clothes for Harper.

Hazel plopped the bags that she'd been holding onto the floor at her feet. "Nah, I think she can still buy another boatload of onesies and receiving blankets.

Do you think Lincoln is going to have a fit when he sees the bill?"

I doubted it. Harper had a lucrative movie career before abandoning it for Lincoln and motherhood. "He might freak out when he sees how much stuff a baby requires, but it's not like this all just happened. I mean, they bought a crib last month, and the guys helped put it together," I said.

That aside, it was still a surprise. Harper hadn't expected to get pregnant, and while she and Lincoln were excited to welcome a baby in a few weeks, it hadn't been planned.

"Can I ride the rocket?" Izzie pointed at the machine tucked into the corner of the mall.

I dug into my pocket to see if I had any quarters to feed the machine. "Sure. Can you watch the bags?" I didn't expect Hazel to abandon them and disappear, but I thought that I should still politely ask.

"Yes, go. Have fun!" She waved us off, and Izzie tore off toward the rocket.

I hurried after Izzie. She had already climbed into the seat and waited for me to feed the device.

I dropped several quarters in and watched as it came to life.

The rocket lit up and made several sounds before bouncing wildly, earning a fit of giggles from Izzie.

She was easy to entertain today.

Harper waddled down the hall from the bathroom and met up with Hazel by the bench. She waved at Izzie and me before she sat beside Hazel.

The two girls chatted animatedly, laughing and gossiping about who knows what.

I turned my attention back to Izzie, only to find her gone.

The rocket ended its jittering, and I poked around to the other side, relieved when I found her climb onto a motorcycle. "Again! More quarters?" Izzie asked.

The girl was going to give me a heart attack!

I dropped a few quarters into the motorcycle. The engine made an obnoxious grumble, and the headlights flashed a multitude of colors.

I glanced around the rocket to see Hazel and Harper still engrossed in their conversation.

"This is the last ride," I said to Izzie. "I'm all out of quarters."

She whined in protest and pouted her discontent.

"Psst!"

I glanced behind me.

"Skylar?" I hadn't spoken with her in a while. She'd gotten engaged in secret, and by the looks of it, she seemed to be in trouble. Her hair looked dirty, her skin covered in filth, along with her clothes.

"I need you to come with me," Skylar said. She glanced behind herself at the side exit just a few feet away.

"Izzie, it's time to go." I couldn't leave her alone. I needed to get Hazel and Harper and let them know that something was going on with Skylar. However, I didn't have any idea what the hell it was at the moment.

"No, uh, just you," Skylar said.

"I can't leave her. What's going on, Skylar?" I asked, stepping closer.

"Please, it's a matter of life or death." She slipped out of my reach and tore out the side exit.

Fuck.

I grabbed Izzie and held her on my hip as I jogged toward the side exit.

I pushed open the door.

The bright sunlight momentarily blinded me.

"I'm sorry," Skylar's voice whispered from behind.

A white van parked outside the door. The back door slid open, and my breath caught in my throat when I saw Benjamin Ryan, my ex-husband, on the other side, a gun in his hand.

I reached behind me for the entrance to the mall, the door, my escape.

It was locked from the outside.

"Get in," Ben said, gesturing with the gun to follow his orders.

Slowly, I put Izzie down, planting her feet on the ground. "Run!" I shouted at her, praying that she listened and would go to get help.

I didn't want her tangled up in my mess.

What was Skylar doing with Ben? Since when had they become friends?

Izzie clutched to my side, unwilling to run to save herself.

He cocked off the safety of the gun and pointed it at the little brunette's head. "Get in, or she dies!"

CHAPTER FOURTEEN

Skylar

Running had seemed a grand idea, until the gunshot had gone off.

I didn't want to die.

Not today.

Escaping seemed the only option when faced with exploitation. Why had Enzo betrayed Jayden and me?

He'd handed me over to the enemy without a second thought.

My fingers grazed the ribbon that Enzo had tied into my hair. It had been a strange gesture. I yanked it hard, wanting no evidence of him on me.

The dress I wore, he gave me that too.

My stomach sunk. I was going to be sick.

I couldn't disrobe. I had nothing else to wear.

Had Enzo intentionally been trying to mark me?

Claim me? Show me that I belonged to him?

In the back of the SUV, I pulled my hair down, letting the long locks fall around my face. The bobby pins and clips, I dropped on the floor.

Inside the red ribbon, had been the tiniest message, meant only for my eyes.

Get information if you want to survive. You work for us now.

I was furious.

Had Jayden been in on the scheme, or had it been Don Ricci's idea? Jayden hadn't so much as mentioned it, and he had looked pretty shaken when he'd been detained and I'd been thrust in front of the crowd.

If I wanted to survive, I had to obey Don DeLuca's every command, at least until help arrived.

Would someone come and save me?

Jayden wasn't my fiancé, not really. We had pretended to be engaged to be married, and that had been short-lived. Sadly, it lasted longer than any of my real relationships.

Pathetic, I know.

Jayden's backup plan for me to flirt with Dante was moot. Angelo DeLuca had dragged me out of Enzo Ricci's home.

Angelo's fist gripped my neck, reminding me that if I didn't do as I was told, I was as good as dead.

I couldn't let anyone see the ribbon. I secured it back up into my hair, making sure that I'd dispose of it properly later. No one could find it. If they did, they'd think I was a spy.

———

I'd been alone, with only a cot, in a cold and moldy basement.

There were other girls. I'd seen them when I'd first been brought down to the basement, past their prison cells.

But I hadn't been able to talk to any of them.

The prison in DeLuca's basement had been quite large, and they brought me to another area, away from the girls who had been locked up together.

Why was I being detained?

Why did he keep me in the farther corner of his prison?

Cement walls and floors with iron wrought bars kept us contained. There was no way to escape, not without a key.

Every so often, I could hear the echo of female voices, but I couldn't hear what they said. It was as if Angelo DeLuca knew why I'd been given to him, and he was keeping me from ever fulfilling my secret mission.

Would Jayden come for me?

What about Enzo Ricci?

———

Heavy footfalls thumped over the floor.

I sat up, waiting to see who was coming in my direction. Was it help? I hadn't heard gunshots or any sound of fighting.

It didn't seem likely that Enzo would show up and Angelo would hand me over to him.

"Well, well, well," Angelo's voice carried into my cell as he rounded the corner. He dressed in slacks and a black button-down shirt. His black hair looked greasy as he slicked it back with too much gel. "Get up!" he commanded.

I stood, folded my arms across my chest, and hesitated as I gradually moved toward the cell door.

Was he going to let me go? He didn't seem the type to give a girl her freedom.

He leered in my direction, glancing every inch of me over. Was he undressing me mentally?

I was parched, and while my body trembled, I hoped that he didn't notice my fear. "What do you want with me?" I asked.

"Tsk. Tsk." Angelo shook his head, unapproving. "I ask the questions. You'll listen."

I wasn't loyal to Enzo or to Angelo. All I cared about was my survival.

The second set of footsteps descended farther down the corridor.

"We know you're the girlfriend of one of Enzo's associates. What I can't fathom is why Don Ricci gave you to us as a gift." Angelo unlocked the cell door and stepped inside, leaving the door ajar.

Could I push past him and make a break for it?

"Any thoughts?" Angelo asked.

The second set of footsteps grew nearer and rounded the corner. I didn't recognize the man. I'm not sure why I thought I might.

It wasn't Jayden. There weren't too many others I knew around here. I was still new to town.

Did Angelo know that about me? He already knew the same story that we'd fed to Enzo about our fake relationship.

Angelo stepped closer when I didn't answer.

I felt trapped, my back against the cold cement wall, leaving me nowhere to go.

Slowly, he lifted a hand. His index finger stroked my cheek. "You're a pretty girl. You might even pass for being honest." He laughed with a darkness that sent a shudder down my spine. "You can rot in this cell or come work for Ben. He needs an associate, and I need more girls."

Ben came to stand on the opposite side of the cell, his arms folded across his chest.

"Are you sure about this?" he asked Angelo.

"If she is intended as a rat, we'll have her working for us, and if she's not, then she'll be indebted to me. I'm giving her a taste of freedom. It comes at a cost," Angelo said.

His finger stroked my jaw before he grabbed my chin and yanked on my face hard, bringing my gaze staring into his cold, lifeless eyes.

I held my breath.

"Disobey any of my men, and they will put a bullet in your head. Then, we'll hunt down your pretty little boyfriend," Angelo said.

He released his tight grip on my face, and I breathed a sigh, though I didn't feel relieved, not yet. It was far from over.

"I want you back here by midnight with three girls. They'd better be young, fresh, and full of life." Angelo shot Ben a hard glare.

There was something unsaid between them.

A heaviness hung in the air.

Was it about me?

"Let's go," Ben grunted, and pointed at the hallway.

Wordlessly, I stepped out of the prison cell and followed Ben down the narrow hallway. I kept my head down. I didn't want to be here, and I sure as hell didn't want to get myself further involved in this mess.

I needed a plan, and I needed one fast.

Abduct three girls by midnight?

If I wasn't going to jail, I'd be going to Hell.

CHAPTER FIFTEEN

ARIELLA

Izzie clung to me. I held her tight, her arms wrapped around my chest as I reluctantly climbed into the back of the van.

While I was willing to risk my life, I wasn't willing to endanger Izzie.

I knew she was afraid, but I wished she'd have done as I asked and ran. At least she could have saved herself.

The back door, the exit we had been whisked out of, squeaked open.

Hazel and Harper stepped outside.

Shit.

I opened my mouth to scream, to warn them to run back inside and get help.

But it was too late.

"You!" Ben's eyes narrowed and he snarled at the two of them. "Get in!" he barked at both of them, waving a gun at Harper's pregnant belly.

Harper held up her hands. "Okay. Okay. Don't shoot us!" She waddled toward the white van. A look of fear crossed her face when she saw me in the back holding Izzie.

Did he know that Harper, Hazel, and I were friends? What did he want with them?

Hazel hesitated.

"Get in or I'll shoot the little girl." Ben whipped the gun around to point it at Izzie.

Hazel huffed under her breath but climbed into the back of the van, coming to sit beside me. She rested a hand on my leg as we all sat curled up on the floor.

Skylar climbed in with us before Ben slammed the van door shut.

A moment later, the engine roared to life. Where was he taking us? If he was after me, why involve everyone else?

"What the hell were you thinking?" I shot at Skylar as she sat on the floor across from us. Why was Skylar friends with Ben?

"I didn't have a choice," Skylar said, her eyes bent down on the metal floor of the truck.

Harper rested a hand over her pregnant belly. "Doesn't matter. We're in this situation now. What are we going to do about it?"

Ben couldn't hear us from the front seat as he drove.

I tried the door handle, not that I expected it to open. Even if it did, what would we do? Jump out of a moving van? We had a child and a pregnant woman, so that didn't seem the best plan.

I pulled out my cell phone from my pocket. Ben clearly wasn't versed in kidnappings. Thankfully, he hadn't learned much from the last time he'd abducted me.

"Where is he taking us?" I asked, staring at Skylar.

She sat with her legs crossed, gnawing on her bottom lip.

Great. Skylar wasn't going to help.

I pulled up Jaxson's number and tried calling him.

It rang and went to voicemail.

Seriously? What was he doing that was so important? Although he wouldn't have known we'd been tossed into the back of a van.

"Jaxson, your crazy ass sister got the four of us abducted by Benjamin Ryan. We're in the back of his white van and, according to GPS, heading northeast. I don't know how long we'll have our phones. Please call us."

"Daddy," Izzie said, reaching for my phone.

I hung up the call. "I'm sorry, sweetie, Daddy didn't pick up." I turned my phone on silent and shoved my phone into my fashionable boots.

Izzie trembled in my arms and clung to me even tighter, her hold making it hard to breathe.

Gently, I caressed her back, trying to ease her fears. The girl had been through enough already in her short lifetime.

Skylar stared at Izzie. "I'm sorry. It was never my choice to be here, either." Her gaze met my stare. "I know you think Ben is the monster. You probably think I'm one too, but you haven't even come close to discovering what *he's* capable of doing."

"Who?" I asked. If she wasn't referring to Ben, then who was behind our abduction. Who did Ben work for?

"Don DeLuca," Skylar whispered.

I'd barely heard her, and I certainly didn't recognize the name. She kept her stare averted.

Skylar wrung her hands together before she focused on her fingernails and picked away at the light pink nail polish.

"Is that name supposed to mean something to me?" I asked. I glanced at Hazel and Harper. Not that I expected them to recognize the name, but maybe they were aware of something I hadn't been knowledgeable about.

"Shit," Harper whispered.

"What?" I glanced at her. What did she know?

"DeLuca works for Don Ricci," Harper said. "Well, works for is a strong term. After I discovered Enzo's background, I did a little digging."

"Digging?" I asked.

"Yes, I hired a private investigator to find out who I was married to and why he'd been in Vegas. When I saw on the news that Enzo was wanted for a slew of crimes, I thought he was the only mob boss."

"Mob boss?" Hazel whispered. "If they know my last is Agron, they'll kill me." She pulled her knees to her chest, her eyes wide. I could feel her tremble beside me in the van.

Hazel's eldest brother was head of the Russian mob in Chicago, but he was dead. We hadn't kept up with who had risen in power, but Hazel was likely still a target of the Russian mafia. They'd left her alone after her betrothed, Franco Ivanov, had been arrested, but that didn't mean they weren't out for getting revenge if DeLuca had ties to Chicago.

"Turns out that Angelo DeLuca runs the Nevada and Southwest ring. They're enemies, at least they were. But Lincoln has been keeping tabs on Enzo. He doesn't trust that he'll leave me alone."

Maybe Lincoln was right, and Ben hadn't snatched the four of us because of me. That didn't make me feel the least bit better.

Could it have been because Don DeLuca was trying to get Don Enzo's attention with Harper? Did he think the baby was Enzo's?

"What do we do?" I asked, glancing from Harper to Skylar.

Skylar stared back down at the floor. "I can't help you. Don DeLuca expected three girls by midnight. I didn't have a choice," she whispered. Her voice sounded strained, like she was fighting back the tears.

I'd never seen Skylar cry. She'd been moody and difficult, emotional on a scale of bitchiness. But filled with concern, that wasn't a Skylar who I was familiar with seeing, ever.

The vehicle came to an abrupt halt.

The engine died.

Why were we stopped?

I wanted to grab my phone and glance at the GPS to determine our location, but the van door squeaked and slammed.

Ben was on the move.

Any second, he'd be opening the van door, and I couldn't risk him discovering my phone.

Ben jerked the handle and slid the van door open. "Out!" he demanded, waving his gun at us.

"I want to go home," Izzie said, clutching me tight.

Already, she was in my arms, but her hold on me didn't seem enough. "I know, baby girl." I wanted to go home, too.

I'd lay my life on the line to protect Izzie. She had become as much my daughter as she was Jaxson's.

CHAPTER SIXTEEN

JAXSON

How the hell had I missed her call?

I listened to it again and again. I could hear the fear in her voice, even as Ariella tried to be strong.

They'd gone to the mall. It had to have been where they'd been snatched.

We met up with mall security, a bunch of rent-a-cops, who showed us grainy black and white surveillance footage of the abduction.

Skylar was with them, and Ben definitely had a gun that he pointed at my little girl.

I was going to kill him.

Mason and Lincoln stood at both sides of me, watching the video too. Their girlfriends' lives were on the line, just like my daughters and Ariella's.

It took everything in me not to beat the hell out of Jayden.

He'd caused this mess.

"Call Declan," I rattled off orders. "Have him start pulling surveillance and footage for where Ben might have taken them. Ariella said they were heading northeast. I want Aiden to track her phone. Hell, track all their phones, see if anyone pings a signal. Who the hell is Ben working for?"

"If Skylar is with them, I know who has the girls. They're with Angelo DeLuca," Jayden said.

"DeLuca, as in the crime boss from Vegas? What the hell is he doing in Breckenridge?" I spun around on my heel, coming face-to-face with Jayden, demanding an answer. Suddenly, the name clicked with me.

Lincoln towered over Jayden. "I've been asking myself the same question about Don DeLuca. What is he doing in town? I've had suspicions about him and Enzo. A man like DeLuca doesn't just show up for a nice little vacation in the middle of nowhere," Lincoln said.

Lincoln was right.

DeLuca was up to no good.

"Think it's a turf war?" I asked. Lincoln knew more about the mafia than I did.

I was well aware of his side project in digging into dirt on Enzo Ricci. As much as I wasn't keen on it, I didn't think his private investigative work was the reason that the girls had been snatched.

But I didn't like coincidences.

"No," Lincoln shook his head. "I have it on good authority that they're doing business together."

Fuck. That was news to me.

It wasn't bad enough Enzo Ricci had moved into Breckenridge, but now we had to deal with Angelo DeLuca as well? "What kind of business?" I shot a glance back at Jayden. "You know what this is about, don't you?"

He had kept quiet for far too long.

I was ready to get my hands dirty and torture the bastard if it meant finding my daughter and getting her and the girls back.

Jayden took a step back in the small confines of the mall security room.

I cleared my throat. The mall security officers didn't need any more intel than we'd already provided them.

"How about we take it outside?" I asked. It wasn't a question.

The guys headed out of the mall security office and through the double doors outside.

"Listen." Jayden held up his arms in surrender.

He was probably worried we'd all pound the shit out of him.

It certainly crossed my mind, but he was far more useful to us alive and unharmed.

"I didn't mean for any of this to happen. You have to know that I wouldn't ever get involved in hurting a pregnant woman or a kid," Jayden said with insistence. "I want to help. Let me talk to Enzo and see if we can get DeLuca to turn over the girls and the kid."

Mason's scowl hadn't left his face. "Do you honestly think putting Enzo in the middle of this is going to help anyone? We don't need to get indebted to a mobster. We'll handle it Eagle Tactical style," Mason said.

"If you mean we go in guns blazing and blow-up DeLuca's compound, I'm all for it," Lincoln said.

I had no objections. We needed to act quickly.

I headed outside for the truck, the guys falling in step just behind me. Our weapons and tactical gear were all back at the Eagle Tactical office.

Besides, we needed blueprints or some type of schematics so that we weren't going in blind.

It would take time to devise a foolproof plan, a commodity that we didn't have a lot of considering what we were up against.

We hightailed it back to the office where Declan and Aiden were busy doing research, trying to track the girls' phones and getting us access to security footage inside DeLuca's compound.

Lucy, the receptionist, jumped up the moment we came inside. "I'm so sorry. I just heard what happened," she said, following us down the hall. "If there's anything I can do to help. I know how much your daughter means to you, sir."

I exhaled a heavy breath. It wasn't just Izzie missing, although she was at the forefront of my mind.

Ariella had also been taken, and given her medical condition, I wasn't too keen on her being detained by a mobster. Not that I was happy any of the girls had been abducted at gunpoint.

"That's appreciated, Lucy," I said.

I recognized that she wanted to help. It was why she wasn't hidden behind her desk and was actually taking an active role in what we did for a living.

But I couldn't involve her or put her life at risk. She wasn't former military. Lucy had no tactical training. She was well versed in answering the phone, making appointments, and keeping the office stocked.

I probably sounded like an ungrateful ass. Yes, I was grateful for Lucy's offer to help, but I wasn't going to risk her life to save the girls.

In all honesty, there was nothing that she could do.

"Guys," Aiden's voice carried through the hall.

I hurried with a brisk pace to his office and poked my head inside. "You got something?" I hoped he wasn't just telling us hello.

My heart was like a jackhammer, pounding against the torn pavement. I felt on edge, ready to scream and unleash a fury that I hadn't known I harbored until today.

My baby girl was in danger.

Ariella was in danger.

The two people in the world who mattered the most to me could die today.

It wasn't a thought I could handle or a reality I was ready to live with.

"I got a ping off one of the phones, Ariella's," Aiden said. "It was brief and only lasted a second, but we've got the vicinity narrowed down."

Declan carried his laptop into the office and joined us, along with Mason and Lincoln.

"Jayden's convinced they're being held at Angelo DeLuca's compound," I said. I caught him up to speed with what he and Declan had missed.

Jayden hung out in the hallway, his arms folded. He appeared remorseful but uncomfortable. Probably because we were prepared to string him up by the balls if anything happened to any of the girls who had been kidnapped.

"You should see this," Declan said. He had hacked into surveillance footage for DeLuca's residence, which also happened to be the location of his compound.

He tapped the screen and zoomed in, cleaning up some of the video surveillance footage.

A little girl tore up the wooden staircase alone. "That's Izzie!"

Had she gotten away from the men?

Why was she running upstairs and not out the door?

"We need to move, now!" I couldn't watch and witness something horrific happen to my daughter.

I whisked out of the room for the door. "Call me as soon as you have something concrete!"

Jayden took off after me. "I'm coming with you. I got your families into this mess. I'll get them out of it."

I shot him a glance. I didn't know what he had planned, but we were likely going to need a distraction. For all I cared, Jayden could be the bait.

CHAPTER SEVENTEEN

Skylar

I never had a plan, not when Don DeLuca demanded that I help his associate nab three girls by midnight.

Running might have been the better option, but I wasn't one to flee. Besides, where would I have gone that wouldn't have wound up with me shot dead and tossed into the forest?

Ben had insisted we do the kidnapping at the mall.

He was an idiot.

I couldn't believe he wanted us to grab three girls while on camera. Was he trying to get us caught?

Maybe he wanted me tossed in jail, and he planned on driving away, leaving my ass behind.

I put nothing past him.

We weren't friends.

I didn't even like the bastard.

Would Jayden come for me? I doubted that I'd happen to run into him. That was too big of a coincidence, and I didn't so much as have my cell phone on me that he could track.

I'd done as instructed, stalked into the mall and, upon seeing Ariella, I had hoped that I could involve her, if only for her help.

Having lived with her and Jaxson for the past few months, I knew her secret. Ariella had once been a C.I.A. operative. Well, I knew she worked for the C.I.A.

I wasn't exactly sure what she did, but if anyone had training and could get us out of this mess, Ariella was smart, cunning, and had been through enough hostage situations that she had to be prepared this time.

Right?

Boy, was I wrong.

Fuck me.

I still couldn't get over the fact Izzie came chasing after us.

Don't get me wrong. I hate kids. I plan never to have any, but she's my niece, and as much as she's a snotty toddler, she's also my kin.

Why couldn't she have listened to Ariella when she told her to run?

I should have done something.

I could have fought Ben, helped her get away, and aid in my own escape, too.

But I'd been foolish and selfish. The truth was I was afraid that Ben would kill me, or worse, the little girl he'd pointed the gun at.

And so I'd done what I'd been told, sheepishly climbed into the van and prayed that one day Ariella and Jaxson would find it in their hearts to forgive me.

Today, wasn't going to be that day.

"Get out!" Ben shouted at us, waving his gun.

This time he wasn't alone.

He'd parked the van by the back entrance of the compound, and DeLuca's men held their guns, reminding us to obey their commands.

No one wanted to climb out of the van first, least of all me.

The girls didn't budge, and I'd been here long enough to know that if we didn't follow their instruction, there would be consequences.

Exhaling a loud huff, I climbed out of the van first and, without so much as looking, could hear the commotion behind me as the other girls followed.

"Follow me," Ben said and led us in through the metal door and down the stairs toward the basement. "Not you. You stay here," he instructed Skylar.

"Where are you taking her?" Ariella asked.

Did she still care about me after what I'd done?

Her glance toward me was brief as she clutched Izzie tight to her chest, holding the little girl in her arms. Maybe I imagined it, but she didn't look angry like I would have expected.

Was it disappointment? Perhaps sadness.

Or I just didn't want to see that she hated me. That was as much a real possibility.

"That's none of your concern," Ben said.

"Who's the kid? We haven't been apart long enough for her to be yours," Ben said.

He reached for Izzie, prying her from Ariella's grip.

"No!" Ariella shifted her body, protecting my niece from his grabby hands.

"What do you want with her?" I asked. "She's just a kid."

I didn't know what Ben planned to do with the girls, but I suspected it wasn't good. I'd seen the handful of women in the basement, and from what I'd gathered previously from Jayden, they were being trafficked.

"Fine. You want her. She's your responsibility," Ben said as he shoved Izzie into my arms.

Shit.

What did I know about kids?

Izzie's eyes filled with tears and her bottom lip trembled before the dam broke. "I want my Daddy!" Izzie wailed, squirming in my arms.

She didn't want me to hold her, not that I blamed her. We weren't best friends. She probably knew I wasn't keen on her, and she obviously was making it clear she didn't want to be stuck with me, either.

"You're going to be fine," Ariella said, gently rubbing Izzie's back. "Skylar isn't going to let anything happen to you. Isn't that right?"

The look she shot me sent a shiver down my spine.

"Yes, that's right. You're safe with me," I said, holding Izzie on my hip.

I wanted to put her down. I wasn't used to holding a kid, let alone thirty or maybe forty pounds that had latched itself around my neck and hips.

The kid had no intention of loosening her grasp on me.

"You'll protect her, at all costs," Ariella said and leaned in close to my ear. "Or so help me, I will hunt you down and make you suffer Jaxson's wrath."

Ariella was right. I feared my older brother far more than I feared her.

CHAPTER EIGHTEEN

ARIELLA

Jaxson was going to kill me.

The scum-sucking vermin had snatched Izzie right out of my arms and handed her over to Skylar.

Jaxson's sister didn't look the least bit pleased to have to take charge of the little girl.

Ben led Skylar away from us, up another set of stairs and out of sight.

"Momma!" Izzie screamed.

Was she calling for me?

I hated the fact that Ben was up there with Izzie and Skylar. Anyone else, and I'd have been afraid but not like this. I knew what Ben was capable of.

He was a monster.

Ben had abducted me, threatened me, held me captive, and would have killed me if given a chance.

My heart ached and my stomach sank.

Was he going to hurt Izzie to get back at me for what I'd done all those years ago?

I may not have been Izzie's biological mother, but I was the only mother Izzie had known. Emma, her biological mother, was out of the picture, in prison. She hadn't wanted her daughter and had intended on giving her up for adoption.

"Move!" a man I didn't recognize commanded. He had thick, bushy eyebrows and short, dark curly hair.

He led Hazel, Harper, and me down a set of stairs, a gun poised at us to remind us that he was in charge.

"Hurry up!" the man commanded as we stepped down into the dim basement.

Row after row of prison cells lined the underground compound. To the right, several women were locked inside one of the cells.

He unlocked the second prison cell, and the iron-clad door squeaked open as he swung the door outward.

"Get in," he said, gesturing with his gun for us to do as he instructed.

I glanced over my shoulder at Hazel and Harper in the rear. Behind them, two guards stood armed with semi-automatic weapons.

There were too many of them, and Harper was pregnant. I couldn't fight them without risking too much.

I hesitated before I did as I was told. I stepped into the prison cell. Hazel followed just a few steps behind me.

"Please, sir," Harper said, a hand on her oversized belly. There was no hiding the fact that she was pregnant from these men.

She stood at the entrance to our cell but hadn't stepped inside yet.

"Move!" he shouted and shoved Harper in past the iron gates.

She stumbled forward, tripping over her swollen feet.

I rushed forward and reached out to catch Harper and keep her from falling onto the ground. We needed to get out of this situation unscathed.

He stood blocking the exit, but he hadn't yet shut the metal doors, locking us inside.

"Give me your phones."

Hazel and Harper slowly dug into their pockets, retrieving their devices.

I didn't budge from where I stood on the cement floor. "Mine fell out when we were picked up," I said, doing my best to lie. I refused to back down, my eyes staring into his.

If I so much as flinched, he might see through the charade.

His eyes narrowed as his eyes raked over my body. "I don't believe you. Strip down."

"I swear, I don't have my phone." I held up my hands in surrender. "You can search me," I said. I hoped that would suffice.

I didn't want to strip down, least of all for him.

Thankfully, Skylar had already been shuffled away or she might have given up the location of my cell phone.

She was the last person I trusted, well, her and Ben.

Were they working together, or had she gotten herself involved inadvertently? They weren't keeping her in prison with us.

The man with the bushy eyebrows stepped toward me.

His breath smelled of stale coffee, and he wreaked of day-old cigarette smoke. "Arms out," he commanded.

I held out my arms while he patted me down a little too intimately. With one hand, his fingers cupped my breasts, fondling them in the process before he shoved his hand inside the waistband of my jeans.

"Please, stop." My voice caught in my throat.

Bile rose to my lips. I swallowed down the burning liquid and pinched my eyes shut.

He lifted his hand with the gun, placing the barrel against my forehead. "I give the orders. Don't ever forget that."

His fingers grazed over my panties.

My stomach flopped and my body trembled.

He yanked his hand out of my pants.

"Turn around."

Was it over?

His hand did the same dance over my buttocks, inside the waistband of my jeans, before he withdrew his hand away and lowered the gun.

A moment later, he stalked to the door, stepped out, and closed the iron bars. The metal squeaked as he latched the lock.

Once he was gone, out of sight, I collapsed onto the cold cement floor.

I didn't feel cold.

My body was numb from the inside, and the tremors took over every ounce of my existence. I sat with my legs pulled up to my chest, shaking uncontrollably.

Hazel bent down and rested a hand on my back.

"We'll figure this out," she said, her voice soft and comforting.

I nodded solemnly and glanced toward the hallway. There were no guards standing in wait. Perhaps because we were behind bars, they no longer considered us a threat.

With a quick glance around the room, I recognized no surveillance equipment. There were no signs of cameras and recording devices, although I wasn't sure if they were listening to us.

I'd have to be careful.

Slowly, I withdrew my cell phone from my boot.

I lifted my finger to my lips, warning the other girls in the next cell over not to say anything as they watched us with a fierce intensity.

Would they betray us?

We were all in this together, right? Unless one of them had been like Skylar, hired by the mob to kidnap women.

Was that what happened with Skylar, or had I gotten it all wrong? Did it matter? She'd led us into the hands of the mob. And for what purpose?

I retrieved my cell phone from my boot and glanced at the signal.

No service.

That was strange.

Just about everywhere that I'd been in, Breckenridge had cell service. While the signal might not have been strong in the mountains, there had been plenty of cell towers.

They were probably blocking the signal. But if I could just get outside with my phone, then I could reach Jaxson and he could track me.

That was an unrealistic expectation.

Why would they let me outside?

And if I could get outside, I'd sure as hell run far and fast. I wasn't going to stick around to make a call.

Hopefully, Jaxson was able to locate the signal before we were tossed into the compound.

"Nothing," I said and shoved my phone back into my boot. As long as they'd already searched me, hopefully, they wouldn't go looking again for the device.

———

Gunfire erupted in the distance.

Was that Jaxson and the team coming to rescue us?

The lights flickered in the basement, and the three of us sat huddled together on the floor.

"We move the girls, now!" Ben's voice echoed as he hurried down the basement stairs.

Behind him, a half-dozen men with guns ushered us out of the prison cells and to follow them outside.

Hazel and I quickly stood and helped Harper to her feet.

"She stays," the man with the bushy eyebrows said, pointing at Harper.

"Are you sure?" Ben asked the other man. "We could get double for her."

"These men don't want babies. They want sex. I'll make some calls, see if we can find a buyer outside of our usual channels."

"No," I said and stepped in front of Harper.

Was I helping her or making things worse by leaving her behind with these monsters?

I wanted to protect Harper, but I felt the barrel of Ben's gun against my head. I heard the click of the safety being turned off.

"Don't tempt me, sweetheart," he said, his breath against my ear as he leaned in and grabbed my arm.

CHAPTER NINETEEN

Jayden

I'd sworn to myself that I'd never work with the guys from Eagle Tactical.

Why?

Because I already owed them my life.

We'd served together in the military. Jaxson had pulled my ass out from behind enemy lines while I'd been shot, bleeding to death.

I should have died.

He should have left me to die.

Thanking him seemed inadequate after he risked his life, bullets flying at him. He'd been reckless but selfless.

I wasn't deserving.

He threw himself on the line. He could have died, and I owed him.

What did I do when we returned home?

I kept my distance.

I might have owed Jaxson my life, but I wasn't going to risk his, not when my niece's life was on the line. He'd already done more for me than I deserved. I couldn't involve him. It was my burden to bear.

He had a kid, a daughter at home. It was no secret that he was a single father.

I wouldn't risk his daughter not growing up with a father, alone in the world.

And so, every time he offered me a gig with Eagle Tactical, I turned him down. It wasn't out of pride. Though he probably thought that was the reason. It's what I made him believe so that I could protect him.

Because deep down, he was still my brother.

Family protected each other.

And now I'd torn his family apart.

I walked the final distance up toward the gate and pressed the buzzer of the wrought-iron gates that protected the property of Don DeLuca.

It was the last place I wanted to be, but Don Ricci had made sure that I got what was coming to me.

Betrayal tasted bitter.

I bite down on my tongue, shoving down any and all emotion that showed conflict. I was doing this to save Skylar.

And I owed Jaxson my life.

"We're even," I said quietly into the microphone that I wore in secret. After this, I no longer owed Jaxson or any of my brothers anything ever again.

"We'll see about that. Head down, be quiet. Quit attracting attention to yourself," Jaxson said.

He was right.

I had to play this carefully. Talking to myself, or rather Jaxson, was going to get me killed.

I didn't want to die. Definitely not today.

I stalked up to the gate and pressed the buzzer. From above, I could spot a guard, gun poised at the tower, ready to shoot.

Hopefully, Don DeLuca didn't shoot first and ask questions later.

"Yes?" A heavy male voice answered the buzz. "Can I help you?"

"My name is Jayden Scott. I'd like to speak with your boss, Angelo DeLuca," I said.

"Don DeLuca isn't taking guests," the voice on the other side of the intercom answered.

"I have information for him regarding Enzo Ricci." I didn't elaborate further.

The lock on the gate clicked, and the iron fence separated, allowing me access to enter.

I stepped forward and walked the length of the driveway up toward DeLuca's compound.

It took every ounce of strength not to glance to my left and right, where, in the distance, Jaxson and his team snuck onto the premises.

Bang!

I ducked, hearing a bullet whiz by my head.

What the hell? Who was shooting at me? Eagle Tactical or DeLuca's men?

The sound of gunfire erupted all around me.

"I'm under heavy fire," Mason's voice filled my earpiece.

"On it," Jaxson answered, changing positions. I watched as he tore across the yard by the hedges that sat against the wrought-iron gate.

He shot off several rounds, taking out the guy who had been shooting at Mason.

Gunshots erupted from all around. I was a giant target with no place for cover at my current position.

I rushed to the front entrance as I pulled my pistol from its holster at my hip.

"I'm heading inside," I announced to the team.

"No, I'm going through the west entrance," Lincoln said as he scaled the building and climbed up to the balcony. "They'll expect us to come in the front door."

We had gone over the plan, with Lincoln sneaking up the ivy on the side of the property. I was supposed to waltz through the front door, invited.

It seemed the plan had changed.

"Jayden, your cover's been blown. Stay outside with Mason. I'm heading in with Lincoln to find and recover the girls," Jaxson said.

I kept my position, shooting at DeLuca's men as they headed for the front door. I wasn't letting them step outside.

Gunfire erupted at every position all around us.

From inside, shots were fired.

What the hell was going on in there?

CHAPTER TWENTY

ARIELLA

Ben yanked me forward and out of the cell, in line behind the other girls who were in the next prison cell beside us.

We hadn't said much to them.

The sound of gunfire grew louder and nearer.

Was it Jaxson?

Had the guys from Eagle Tactical come to save us?

I wanted to stay, to fight, to see if we could stall and help aid in our rescue, but with the gun against my skin and Ben trigger happy, I was out of options.

We were marched up the back stairwell, the same way that we came in. Ushered outside, I glanced at Hazel and hoped that she had the same idea I had.

Now was the time to fight.

I thrust my elbow at Ben, landing a blow to his stomach and then his face, feeling his nose crack under my fist.

The other girls gasped and stood frozen.

They didn't fight.

They didn't run.

They stood there, trembling out of fear.

I couldn't count on them to help.

Where was Jaxson?

The gunfire erupted on the opposite side of the compound. Several additional shots were inside.

Was Harper all right? What about Izzie?

Ben grabbed me by the hair and dragged me the remainder of the distance to the van. He tossed me inside, and the other girls silently followed.

"Move!"

Hazel climbed in last. Her bottom lip trembled as she came to sit beside me, cuddling up against me.

Ben slammed the van door shut and the engine roared to life. The vehicle jolted forward as we were whisked off the premises.

Where the hell were they taking us?

CHAPTER TWENTY-ONE

JAXSON

I climbed the trellis of ivy up the side of the compound.

We had to move quickly.

Lincoln was already upstairs, staking out the place, making sure we were clear.

Gunfire erupted as I breached the window and threw myself inside. I couldn't shoot. I could barely cover myself as I flung my body through the small space.

Lincoln covered me.

Two men of DeLuca's lay in a pool of their own blood, dead.

"We need to move," Lincoln said.

I leaped to my feet, gun poised and ready to go. The tactical gear weighed us down and had made it a little more uncomfortable to climb the ivy and whisk me in through the window.

"On it," I answered. I followed behind Lincoln as he had already scoped out the room and made sure it was safe where we'd entered.

Together, we exited the small bedroom and flanked into the hallway.

"Upstairs!" a gruff voice shouted.

Several pairs of boots trampled up the steps in haste.

"Reinforcements," I muttered under my breath to Lincoln.

We positioned ourselves around the edge of the banister, careful not to be seen. As DeLuca's men tore up the stairs, shooting blindly, we landed shot after shot at their heads for a kill shot.

We didn't come to take prisoners. We were here on a search and recovery mission.

Anyone standing in our way was the enemy.

The compound was at least two stories. I suspected there also might have been a basement. The girls could have been kept anywhere.

Room to room, we searched the premises, just the two of us. The majority of the rooms upstairs were empty.

Additional gunshots erupted outside.

"We need to move," I said. We had to hurry. It wouldn't be long until more men tore up the stairs looking for us. We'd shot down the half-dozen soldiers who had come for retribution.

Lincoln opened door after door, and I went with him, gun drawn, prepared to take out anyone who stood in the way of finding our families.

Yanking the door open, I stared at Izzie as she sat at a child's table with Skylar and a teen girl having a tea party.

"Daddy!" Izzie shouted. She leaped out of her chair. The tiny wooden seat fell to the floor as she rushed across the room.

"Don't move," DeLuca's voice echoed from behind.

I heard the click of the safety being turned off as I felt the barrel of the gun at the back of my head.

CHAPTER TWENTY-TWO

ARIELLA

"You okay?" I whispered to Hazel.

We sat huddled together in the back of a van. Darkness surrounded us.

There were more than just the two of us. Nearly a dozen women had been crammed inside the back of the white van, the same vehicle we were brought in with, just a short while ago.

"No," Hazel muttered. "None of this is okay."

I knew that.

"We'll get out of this alive," I said.

"How?" Hazel asked. "As sex slaves? I'd rather take a bullet to my head."

"Don't talk like that," I said. "We do what we have to for survival. We can fight these men. As far as I can tell, there's only one driving us. When we get to wherever they're taking us, we fight."

"That won't work," another girl said. I didn't recognize her voice. It was raspy and thick. She sounded parched. "You fight, you get tied up, beaten, raped, the list goes on. The men, they all take turns, and we all have to watch."

"How long have you been with these men?" I asked.

I wasn't sure I wanted to know, but it was clear she'd been around for a while to witness what transpired when the prisoners fought back.

"Not long, a few weeks. Some of the girls have been shuffled between families. Bought, used, and sold like garbage. That's how they treat us, and you're lucky if their interest is sexual and not masochistic," she said.

A shiver ran through me.

"Being forced to marry Franco Ivanov, suddenly sounds like a picnic," Hazel muttered.

I wrapped an arm around her shoulder, trying to reassure her as best I could that we would get out of this alive.

I just wasn't sure how.

———

With a gun poised at your temple, there's no way to fight back.

Two men stood guard outside of the van. One held a gun at our heads while we climbed out of the vehicle, the other secured a collar to each of our necks.

A third guard waited just a few feet away, a black remote in his palm.

"No one's going to fight back?" he asked with a chuckle and tilted his head. "That's too bad." He pressed down on the button, forcing a jolt of electricity to run through all of our bodies at the same time.

I fell to the ground. My eyes squeezed shut.

Everything inside of me ached like lightning burned through my veins. I gasped for breath. My heart hammered in my chest.

The electricity lasted only a few seconds, but it felt like forever.

"There will be no insubordination," the man said, "or you all will suffer the price."

We were connected. All of us, forced to endure torture together.

The collars were their method of control. There was no way to escape.

CHAPTER TWENTY-THREE

JAXSON

"Don't shoot, Angelo," I said, holding my hands up.

"It's Don DeLuca to you," Angelo said.

"I'm on it," Mason said through the earpiece.

Good, he'd gotten the message that we were in trouble and needed additional backup.

I hoped he'd come in time.

Lincoln refused to lower his gun as he pointed it across the room at Angelo. He closed the distance as he stepped forward.

"Don't hurt him!" Skylar jumped up from her seat at the table, where she'd been having tea with Izzie and the teen girl.

"What are you doing?" Don DeLuca's eyes narrowed as he studied the young woman.

"Izzie, come here," Skylar said, holding out her arms, trying to protect my daughter from DeLuca.

My daughter's eyes watered as she glanced from Skylar and then back to me. Her bottom lip trembled.

"Go with Skylar," I said, trying desperately to protect my baby girl.

It was clear Izzie wasn't sure what to do.

I needed to protect her, and it was difficult with the barrel of a gun against the back of my head.

"Time's up," Mason's voice echoed from behind DeLuca as he stood in the hallway. "You'll let them go, or I'll end your inconsequential life."

"Shoot me," DeLuca said. "Do you honestly think it's over? Your girls, they're gone."

Skylar grabbed Izzie and pulled her safely out of harm's way, behind her legs, shielding her from danger.

Mason yanked a pair of metal handcuffs from his belt loop and thrust DeLuca's hands behind his back, securing his wrists in place.

"What do you mean, they're gone?" Lincoln seethed.

Izzie rushed past Skylar for me, arms raised.

I pulled her into my arms, cuddling her for only a moment. I wanted to relish the moment, reassure her that everything was fine and she was safe, but we weren't home.

There could have been countless other men ready to take aim.

I was just hoping Izzie was no longer in danger.

Where were the others?

Where were Ariella, Hazel, and Harper?

———

With DeLuca detained, we searched the compound, shooting anyone garnishing a weapon.

Most of his men fled. The few who had stayed, we'd gunned down. They hadn't given us another option.

With our guns raised, we headed down the stairs for the basement.

DeLuca accompanied us, arms bound behind his back with metal cuffs. Skylar, Izzie, and the teenage girl stood with Mason, keeping guard, protecting them in case Angelo tried anything stupid.

"There's no one down here. I'm telling you, the girls are gone," DeLuca said.

He didn't appear the least bit apologetic or contrite.

"How about we see for ourselves?" I led the way, gun drawn, making sure there were no more men brandishing weapons.

"Help!" Harper's voice carried from down in the basement.

"Harper?" Lincoln hurried past me for the prison cell, as I made sure there were no other guards hidden in the basement lockup.

The hallway twisted and turned.

The overhead fluorescent bulbs flickered and sizzled.

I glanced past the empty prison cells and reached the end before turning around to come back and join them.

Lincoln grabbed a pair of keys that hung on the opposite wall and unlocked the metal door. He helped Harper to her feet, examining her with a quick gaze. "Here, let me help you up." He offered her his hand.

"I told you they left," DeLuca said. "They're not coming back to the facility. At least the girls aren't." He quirked a sly grin.

My stomach flopped, and I lurched forward, yanking him by his hair, my gun poised at his chin, pointed upward.

"Where did you send them?"

Ariella and Hazel were still out there and, by now, could be anywhere.

I tapped my earpiece, connecting me to Declan and Aiden who were back at the office.

"I need eyes in the sky. We've got Harper, Skylar, and Izzie, but Hazel and Ariella have been taken off the property."

I cocked the safety off on my gun. "You'll tell me where you're taking the girls."

"We came into the compound in a white van," Skylar said.

"We're looking for a white van," I reiterated to Aiden and Declan.

Aiden was a guru with computers, satellite surveillance, and hacking anything and everything, including top-secret government servers. I trusted that he could get us eyes on the van.

"Any idea what direction they headed?" Declan asked.

"Lincoln, take the girls outside. Call in for an ambulance if Harper needs to get checked out," I said.

I didn't want Izzie or the others to witness what I was willing to do to find Ariella.

"Jaxson." Lincoln's voice held a hint of warning. "We've got DeLuca. Why don't we hand him over to the authorities? We could use their assistance in tracking the other girls down."

Of course, Lincoln would want to contact the local sheriff's department, now that we had Harper and she was safe.

I couldn't risk their interference and ruining our operation. We trained for this type of situation and had far more experience than the local Breckenridge sheriff's department.

"Not an option," I said gruffly. "We're doing this on our own."

"What about DeLuca?" Lincoln asked, glancing at him.

"I'll get the information out of him."

While there were some lines I wasn't willing to cross, when it involved my family and my friends, I'd do whatever it took to save them.

CHAPTER TWENTY-FOUR

Jayden

I stood guard out front of the compound.

While I wanted to be inside and helping rescue Skylar and the others, I also recognized that someone had to stand guard and keep a lookout.

If DeLuca's men intended to flee, I wasn't going to let that happen.

The gunfire inside had silenced after quite some time.

I'd have been worried if I hadn't been connected via an earpiece and could hear the conversation amongst the men of Eagle Tactical.

Lincoln stepped outside first, through the front door.

I lowered my gun, careful not to shoot him.

Skylar followed, holding Izzie's hand.

Exhaling a sigh of relief, I was grateful that they were both all right. "I'm glad you're safe," I said.

Skylar dropped Izzie's hand and threw back her fist, landing a blow to my face.

"You bastard!" Skylar shouted at me.

Okay, maybe I deserved that. While I hadn't known what Enzo would have done, I shouldn't have ever involved her in my mess. I'd been selfish and irresponsible in bringing a civilian on board.

"You're right. I'm an asshole," I said.

She cocked an eyebrow.

Had she expected me to fight back?

I rubbed my cheek. It stung like hell, but I'd survive. It was nothing an ice pack and a couple of aspirin couldn't cure.

Were my eyes playing tricks on me? Behind Skylar, a young brunette hesitated. Her pale blue eyes stared back at me.

"Lexa!" I shouted to my niece and rushed forward, past Izzie and Skylar.

Lexa threw her arms around my neck. "Uncle Jayden," she whispered before the sobs wreaked havoc on her body.

I caught her in my arms, not letting her collapse to the ground.

"Are you okay?" It was a terrible question, the stupidest that I could have asked, and yet here I was, asking it anyhow.

"We should get the girls into the truck," Lincoln said. "We don't want to be standing out here in case DeLuca brings in reinforcements."

"Affirmative."

Lincoln was good at taking charge and commanding a team. I followed his lead.

Skylar held Izzie's hand and followed behind Lincoln as I wrapped an arm around Lexa, escorting her across the lawn, past the open gate and to the other side, just beyond the road where the truck was parked.

"What about Daddy?" Izzie asked.

"Yeah? Where's Jaxson and Mason?" I asked.

I'd heard briefly over the transmission that they'd stayed behind to interrogate DeLuca. I didn't know what they were capable of outside of a war zone.

Then, again, when one's family was in danger, it meant war.

I'd been down that path looking for Lexa.

"Getting information," Lincoln said. He didn't further elaborate.

We rushed to the vehicle and threw open the back door, letting the girls inside first. Izzie climbed into the back seat with Skylar on one side and Lexa on the opposite.

"I want my daddy," Izzie said. She had trouble sitting still in the backseat.

The kid probably needed a car seat, which was in Jaxson's truck.

"How about we play a game?" Skylar said. "I spy with my little eye something yellow."

"The sun!" Izzie squealed.

Skylar laughed. "Yes, your turn."

Lexa reached for my arm as I stood just outside the truck at the door, keeping watch.

"What's going to happen to me? I mean now that my parents are gone," Lexa asked, her bottom lip trembled.

"You'll come and stay with me," I said.

I had every intention of bringing her home with me. While I might not have known anything about raising a teenager, I wasn't going to send her to foster care or let someone else get their slimy paws on her.

Lexa reached out and wrapped her arms around me for a hug.

She sobbed into my chest.

I wasn't used to girls crying, let alone kids. Well, she was fifteen, not exactly a kid, but still, she needed a role model. And I was the last person on the planet who Lexa should be looking up to.

"I've got you," I said, patting her back as I held her. "I won't let anyone hurt you ever again."

Skylar glanced in my direction. A frown line etched to her brow. She opened her mouth but quickly shut it.

Smiling, Skylar returned her attention back to Izzie and their little game.

"I spy, Daddy!" Izzie squealed. She pointed to Jaxson as he and Mason hurried toward the truck. His hands were covered in blood, his pants just as dirty.

I didn't dare ask what the hell they'd done to DeLuca. The bastard deserved everything he had come to him.

Jaxson was the first to approach the truck. He wiped his filthy hands on his pants, as if that would erase the memories and the bloodshed.

"There's an auction at midnight," Jaxson said. "We need to be there. I've got the GPS coordinates in my phone."

"What about DeLuca?" I asked. "Do we need to worry about him warning his men?"

Mason exhaled a heavy breath. "He's not talking."

CHAPTER TWENTY-FIVE

ARIELLA

I expected to be tossed into a cellar or a basement, behind metal bars on a dingy surface that made me fear my life.

The electric collar pinched my skin. But the men who abducted us brought us inside a home, though it felt more like a fortress.

From the outside, it was heavily guarded, more so than even the last place we'd been taken. While the last prison had been a holding cell, literally keeping us until we reached our next destination, this prison was completely different.

The lights were dimmed as we entered. It took a few moments for my eyes to adjust.

I followed the other girls, keeping close together as the men shoved us forward and through the long hallway and up the staircase.

A dark red carpet led a path up the stairs. My boots sank into the plush material.

Was Jaxson able to track us?

I had to believe that he would come for us, rescue us. It was only a matter of time before we got out of this mess.

A guard opened the door to the right, and we were all ushered inside before the door slammed behind us.

A woman in her mid-seventies stepped out of the shadows, dressed in a pink satin robe. "Come closer," she said, gesturing for us to approach.

When we shuffled slowly, she dug out a small handheld device, the same black remote that the guard had used earlier to shock all of us.

She pressed down on the button, forcing a jolt of pain to sear my neck.

I was doubled over in pain.

Fire burned my skin as I shuddered and fell to my knees. My hands instinctively reached for the collar, but I couldn't remove it.

"I'm Diamond, and remember, ladies, that I do not ask twice," the woman said, a stern expression crossed her face.

Was that even her real name, Diamond?

Had she been one of us once in her life, or was she running the operation?

She held not an ounce of empathy.

We hurried closer, afraid to be zapped again by the madwoman with the remote.

"Very good," Diamond said with a glint in her eye. "You will find this all will go by so quickly and painlessly if you follow my orders the first time."

She paused for a moment and paced slowly, the window behind her. It held cast iron bars, locking us inside.

I imagined the door was locked behind us too. I didn't try to make a break for freedom. It wasn't going to come so easily, not with dozens of armed guards in and around the premises.

"Tonight, you girls will be the most fabulous and precious guests for the evening event. Like me, a diamond, you must shine, sparkle, and gleam. I expect each of you to bathe quickly. After which you will be dressed, and we will do your makeup and hair. Do I hear any objections?" she asked, revealing the black button in her palm.

No one spoke.

"Perfect. Do not be shy. You are the jewels of the evening and, as such, will be passed around to be examined, touched, and thoroughly inspected."

My stomach flopped.

We weren't jewels.

We were people.

And while I appreciated that at least she wasn't calling us sex slaves, that's what we were, being sold into slavery. Any way you diced it, this woman was sick.

The woman pointed at me. "You'll be the first, darling. What is your name?"

I stared at her, unsure of what to say.

She humphed under her breath. "Well, I don't have all day."

"Ariella," I whispered, afraid Diamond might zap me with her twitchy fingers.

Her eyes squinted as she stared at me. Her hand jerked out to grab my jaw as she examined my face from side to side. "That's no good. From this night forward, you are Jade. Now, hurry and get washed up. You need to be presentable for this evening's auction."

I didn't move. My feet were frozen in place.

"Quickly, we haven't got all day," Diamond said.

She snapped her fingers. Thank heavens she didn't press the damned buzzer again.

I hurried across the room to where a guard stood and pointed at the open door.

It led to a connected bathroom with several individual shower stalls. I felt like I was back in college, a lifetime ago.

Hazel was right behind me a few feet. "Apparently, I look like Violet. Why she couldn't let me be Hazel is beyond me," she muttered.

I quirked a grin at her. "She loves purple."

Now wasn't the time to let our guard down. We needed to bide our time but be careful. I needed to strip down, but I wasn't looking forward to bathing around these monsters.

A guard stood at the entrance to the bathroom. There were partitions for each stall, but no curtain and certainly no privacy.

"Do we have to leave this on when we shower?" I asked, pointing at the collar. "I don't want to get zapped from the water."

"The only one zapping you is Madam Diamond herself or one of the ranking guards," the uniformed guard said.

I exhaled a heavy breath but didn't budge from my position in the stall. I'd yet to disrobe.

"Clock's ticking. You have five minutes in here. If you're not sparkly clean at that point, you can bet that necklace will light up like Christmas."

Wonderful.

Slowly, I disrobed, leaving my phone buried inside my boot. What other choice did I have?

It wasn't just a threat. I'd felt the sting of electricity and sure as hell didn't want to feel it again. I'd follow their orders to survive. I just needed to give Jaxson and the Eagle Tactical team a little more time.

They were coming for us, and even if there was a cell phone jammer like the last place, they had to have caught the signal when we were outside or in the van.

I held on to that bit of hope while I stepped forward and turned on the shower spray.

While I couldn't see Hazel because of the frosted tinted partition between us, I could hear her shuffle around as she undressed.

The shower spray warmed, and I stepped under. It was like a rainstorm, pouring down and soaking me from head to toe.

I let the water envelop me as I became one with the shower. I wanted to wash away the filth, the trauma that I'd already endured, but I knew that was foolish.

How could I relax when I was further from being safe?

"Two-minute warning, Jade," the guard said.

Against the wall, was a dispenser for soap and shampoo.

I hurried to clean up the stench that surrounded me. The dirt that covered me was an invisible layer created by Ben and others, like the men standing guard and Diamond with the remote ready to cause pain to anyone she deemed unworthy.

Suds covered me, and just as quickly as the rain shower soaked me, it was over.

The shower shut off without my approval.

The guard shucked a gray towel in my direction. "Dry off and drop your clothes in that bin." He pointed at a giant garbage can by the exit of the bathroom.

Shit, my phone was buried in my shoes.

Well, at least it would stay on unnoticed. I wouldn't be able to secure it on me without being seen. Even with just a towel, the guard hadn't so much as looked away.

Privacy was apparently not in his vocabulary.

I wanted to offer a smartass remark about him taking a picture or if he'd never seen a naked woman before, but I held my tongue. I didn't want to feel Diamond's wrath or force it on the group of girls.

They'd come to hate me if I was the only one fighting back and we all were suffering the consequences.

———

One of Diamond's assistants, her name was Iris, dressed me in a black satin negligee with thin straps that revealed too much cleavage and barely covered my ass.

I felt naked.

That was probably the point.

They hadn't let me put my panties back on, so I kept pulling down the hem of the dress only to have it show more of my breasts.

Wonderful. I was going to be on display for a bunch of pervy men.

My hands trembled, and I tucked them into my arms, folding them across my chest, trying to at least keep some semblance of modesty.

I wasn't the least bit comfortable. And while that should have been the last concern given the men with guns and the collar on my neck, it still was unsettling.

Iris fixed my hair up in curls, pinning part of it up while leaving some long locks in the back.

She did my makeup too, paying extra attention to my eyes and lips.

There wasn't a mirror. I had no idea how I looked, but based on the other girls' appearances, they were going a little too heavy with the eyeliner and lipstick.

I hardly ever wore makeup anyhow, and when I did, it was a little gloss or colored balm for my lips. This felt like overkill.

It had grown dark hours ago.

My stomach grumbled.

The guards had brought in pizza for them to eat, but we weren't given anything more than water.

Were they trying to starve us? Force us into obedience?

We were already following their every command.

The lights dimmed and flickered.

Hazel and I exchanged a brief glance.

"Girls!" Diamond clapped her hands, getting our attention. "It is time to unveil you to our guests. You are to use only the name we've given you tonight. There are cameras everywhere inside and outside of the property. If we so much as suspect any betrayal, you will be punished along with your sisters," Diamond said.

She had us all line up with Hazel and me last in line. I wasn't in any hurry to meet the men downstairs. They were probably men like Ben, wanting to get their dirty hands on us.

Diamond let the other girls step out into the hallway. She stepped in the way of the line, preventing me from walking out before Hazel.

"You two aren't like the other girls," Diamond said. She stepped closer. Her eyes raked over us which sent a chill down my spine.

My hands trembled, but I tried not to let her see.

Hazel and I remained silent.

"Doesn't matter your pasts, backgrounds, what you did to deserve this life," Diamond said. "I shall give you each one piece of advice and use it wisely. Entertain these men tonight, and you may find yourself like me, bathed in fortune."

She reached into her pocket and pulled out a gold bracelet. She grabbed my arm and slipped the metal over my arm, locking it into place. "We will be listening to every word that you speak, Jade," Diamond said.

I swallowed the lump in my throat.

Diamond retrieved a second bracelet and snapped it onto Hazel's wrist.

"Now go. Let the festivities commence," Diamond said. She stepped aside, letting us catch up with the girls as they headed down the stairwell barefoot.

CHAPTER TWENTY-SIX

JAXSON

Heading back to Eagle Tactical, I parked the truck out front.

Mason climbed out first and headed inside to talk to Declan and Aiden. He wanted to know what was going on with Hazel and if they had any new intel since the last time we checked in with them a few minutes earlier.

Lincoln pulled up beside me and killed the engine. "I'm going to swing by the local clinic and have them take a look at Harper."

"I'm fine!" Harper said, waving her hand dismissively at him.

He shot her a look. "You might be, but I need to know our baby is fine too."

Lexa and Jayden climbed out of the backseat. They'd driven back with Lincoln.

"Do you mind if we tag along? Lexa should probably have a doctor examine her."

"I'm fine, Uncle Jayden," Lexa said, rolling her eyes. "I just want to go home, take a hot bubble bath, and relax."

Jayden stalled, probably waiting for one of us to interject.

I unbuckled Izzie from the backseat of my truck and opened the main door. I paused, exhaling a heavy sigh.

I wasn't sure when to do this, to break it to Skylar that her invitation to stay with me was retracted. Now seemed as good a time as any.

"Skylar, you need to find someplace else to crash. You're not coming home with us except to pack your bags."

Skylar's eyes widened. "We're family, Jaxson. You can't kick me out."

"The hell I can't!" My voice grew louder as I spoke. "You just had my daughter and my girlfriend kidnapped. If it were up to me, I never want to see you again." I refused to lower my gaze.

She needed to know what she'd done hurt. It went beyond betrayal. She'd cut my heart and made me bleed.

"I have work to do. We still need to track down Hazel and Ariella. I expect you to clean out your shit and be gone when I get home tonight."

Skylar shoved her hands into her jeans. "If that's what you want."

"I don't trust you, and as long as you're keeping company with him," I said and pointed at Jayden, "you're not welcome in my home."

She opened her mouth to say something, but just as quickly shut it.

Good. I didn't want to hear her lame excuses to justify what she'd done.

I stormed inside the building, leaving Skylar outside without a ride. Jayden or Lincoln could help her if they were so inclined.

It was doubtful that Lincoln would offer Skylar any help.

While they'd been chummy months ago, before he'd fallen for Harper, she'd betrayed him just like she'd betrayed me.

———

Izzie sat at the table where Ariella worked. We'd moved the computer and given Izzie a pencil and a handful of colored pens to doodle with on some blank computer paper.

We weren't prepared for a kid in the office. I didn't have crayons or a coloring book, and while I usually kept those things in a spare bag in the truck, I didn't have it on hand today.

I hadn't planned on going on an excursion.

"Tell me you have something," I said to Aiden.

He tapped away diligently at his keyboard.

Mason stood on the opposite side, arms folded across his chest, his expression solemn, his jaw tight.

"I've got a recent location for Ariella's cell phone, which matches the location that DeLuca gave us," Aiden said.

He scribbled down the information on a piece of paper and handed it to me.

"Thanks," I said gruffly.

"You can't go dressed like that to the auction," Declan said as he waltzed into the office, a fresh cup of coffee in hand. He sipped his mug and stood in the doorjamb.

"What's wrong with the way I'm dressed?" I asked and glanced down at my attire. My dark blue jeans had a streak of blood, and my shirt didn't look any better.

He wasn't wrong. "You have anything I can borrow?" I doubted they kept spare clothes at the office. "Or am I taking the clothes off your back?" I asked.

"You can't go into the auction," Jayden said.

I glanced behind me as he hurried in to catch up with us. Skylar stood by the door, waiting inside, and Lexa kept her company.

"And why the hell not?" I asked.

If anyone was going to rescue Ariella, it was going to be me.

Mason could come too. He'd want to rescue Hazel, and I wasn't going to stop him. Just like I knew he wouldn't stop me.

We were in this together.

"We don't know who is running the auction," Jayden said. "It could be anyone, and you're a prominent name in Breckenridge."

"Everyone knows we work for Eagle Tactical," Mason muttered. "So, what, we just let the girls get bought by some scumbags and then have to mount two rescue missions?" He shook his head and stormed toward Jayden.

"Hey! I'm just trying to help!" Jayden threw his arms up in surrender. "If you want to go and get turned away at the door, then by all means, show up. But if you want someone who can get in and get the girls out, then you need me."

I didn't like whatever plan Jayden had in mind. He was the reason Ariella and Hazel were still missing.

I glanced at the clock on the wall. Time wasn't on our side.

While we could create fake identities and even put on a disguise, it was too risky. These types of events were by invitation only.

"You can get an invitation?" I sized up Jayden.

Jayden nodded eagerly. He was trying too hard. "I know the guy running the auction, Capo Sergio. He's part of DeLuca's family," Jayden said.

Was he trying to make up for what he'd done, or was he hiding something from us?

What choice was there but to trust him?

My phone buzzed in my pocket. Could it be Ariella? I didn't recognize the phone number.

"Hello?" I answered the caller.

"Hi, is this Jaxson?"

"Yes." I felt the guys' eyes on me as I took a step out of the room and stared at Izzie as she quietly colored. She'd managed to get ink all over her hands and on the desk.

"It's Delphine. Ariella was supposed to pick me up from the airport, but she isn't answering her phone."

CHAPTER TWENTY-SEVEN

Jayden

She'd spotted me before I'd even managed to lay eyes on her.

I'd yet to see Ariella, but Hazel sauntered her way over to me, giving me an overly seductive smile.

I tried to play it cool and calm.

Capo Sergio stood beside me. "See anything you like, my man?" he asked, patting me on the back. "You can take her home for the right price."

I cleared my throat. "And what price is that, exactly?" I looked her up and down. I needed to pretend that I was deciding whether she was of interest to me.

"It's a silent auction and cash only. Don't forget that," Sergio said and wagged his finger at me. "I tell you, these girls get hotter, the longer we keep them locked up."

It took everything in me not to slug Capo Sergio. He was the one running this operation, and while I intended to bring it down, I couldn't do it alone.

Wearing a wire had been a discussion, and then turning the information over to the authorities. But I couldn't risk getting caught.

Already, I'd been treading water, barely surviving, between Enzo throwing me out in the cold and handing my fake fiancée over to DeLuca's men.

Sergio probably trusted me as much as I trusted him.

"You can take her for a test drive," Sergio said and gestured with his index finger toward the private rooms. "There is, of course, a fee, but you know how these things are. Anything goes. Nothing is off-limits."

"Good. I'd hate to pay for tainted merchandise," I said. It took everything in me not to vomit, hearing the words leave my lips.

I grabbed Hazel by the hips and pulled her against me. "How much for an hour with her?"

"Twenty minutes, tops. Other prospective buyers should get an opportunity with her too," Sergio said. "Four hundred for twenty minutes."

"Fuck me," I muttered and pulled out four one hundred-dollar bills.

My hand latched onto Hazel's wrist, and I dragged her with a force of intensity toward the private suite and slammed the door behind us.

I wasn't an idiot. There were cameras everywhere. Were there cameras in the private room?

I didn't see any, but that didn't mean anything.

"I'm Violet," Hazel said. Her voice trembled as she took a step back from me.

My eyes tightened as I studied her.

She and the other girls all had black collars around their necks, secured with a metal lock that buckled into place. On her arm, she wore a gold bangle, and she tapped on the bracelet repeatedly as she glanced past me.

Hazel tugged on her bottom lip, bringing it between her teeth, not saying anything further.

"Violet," I said, using the name she'd given me. If she wanted me to know her name wasn't Hazel while we were alone, then she probably thought the men were listening to us.

"Do you understand that I bought your time for the next twenty minutes?" My expression remained cold and dark as I pulled her arm with the bracelet toward me. My fingers fiddled with the bangle while my gaze stayed locked on her eyes.

"Yes, I understand," Hazel said. She stepped closer and climbed onto my lap.

Perhaps she thought they were watching us too?

I didn't think she'd want to be anywhere near me otherwise.

"Suppose I'm interested in buying more than one girl. Is there anyone else who might hold my interest as much as you?" I asked. "I like brunettes with long hair, soulful eyes, with a bit of spark." I had to be careful that no one could decode what we said and make sense of it.

"I, yes, perhaps Jade might be to your liking," Hazel said.

"Good." I smiled, tightlipped.

It'd be a lie to say that I was surprised they required the girls to use different names.

"Tell me, Violet, why might I choose to buy you when I could have any woman in this place?" I asked only because I knew they listened.

She opened her mouth and quickly shut it.

I raised an eyebrow, waiting for her to answer.

Hazel exhaled a heavy breath and leaned closer. Her fingers raked through my hair as her lips reached my ear, whispering so that only I could hear her. "Because if you don't, Mason will hunt you down and kill you."

She wasn't wrong.

———

I had several thousand dollars in cash, most of it on me, but a few grand had been hidden in the truck outside.

I'd been concerned that if all the cash was on me, I could get some of it lifted.

The truth was I had no idea how much it would cost, what a silent auction for a person went for. It wasn't like I could ask someone.

Capo Sergio stood in the center of the room. The lights dimmed, as he had a microphone in his left hand.

"The final moment of the evening you all have been patiently waiting for, the winners of the silent auction," Sergio said.

A wayward smile reached his lips. He received a stack of notecards from an older woman I didn't recognize, dressed in a glittery gold gown that shined like a chandelier under the lights.

"Thank you," Sergio said to her.

The girls were lined up against the wall, and he gestured for the first girl to join him.

"Our first prize of the evening, Ruby, will be going home with Rafael. You may pay me or bring the funds to Diamond to claim your prize." He gestured toward the woman in the gold gown.

Ruby walked to the opposite side of the room beside Diamond.

The young redhead, Ruby, looked downright frightened as she stood waiting for Rafael to complete his transaction.

If I could have saved every girl tonight, I would have, but that wasn't why I came to the auction. I was here for Ariella and Hazel, or rather Jade and Violet.

The auction continued, girl after girl, transaction after transaction.

My stomach flopped as I watched the girls leave, forced to go with a stranger—most of the men, I didn't recognize. However, a few were DeLuca's crew and hadn't been at the compound from what I'd seen earlier in the day.

If they had, I'd have been dead by now.

Thankfully, my cover hadn't been blown.

Did they know Angelo DeLuca was dead? I doubted it was the end of the DeLuca family. Another boss would rise up in his place. Would it be Gino, his second in command?

"Next up this evening, we have Violet. Violet, please step forward," Sergio said as she hesitated to do as told.

She stepped up to the stage and held her breath.

She wasn't the only one. What if I hadn't bid enough to take her home with me? I didn't have any idea how much it cost, and I had to split the amount between Ariella and Hazel.

What if I couldn't afford either one of them?

"Violet, you will be going home this evening with Jayden."

I breathed a sigh of relief. One down.

She crossed the room and headed over toward Diamond, where I was to make the final payment for her to accompany me home.

"And last of the evening, our rare gem, Jade."

I'd barely seen Ariella all night. Had different men bought her time? Had someone else held a firm interest in her?

Capo Sergio glanced down at the card in his hand and shoved it into his back pocket. "Jade will be coming home with me."

CHAPTER TWENTY-EIGHT

JAXSON

"What do you mean, you only got one girl out? We gave you enough money to pay for both Ariella and Hazel."

This could not be happening!

The room spun, and I pinched my eyes shut.

While I was relieved Hazel was safe and reuniting with Mason any minute now, I was sick to my stomach thinking about what would happen to Ariella.

I shouldn't have gone home. Aiden and Declan talked me into taking Izzie home.

I should never have left Jayden to handle the operation.

"Capo Sergio, the bastard who runs the auction, he kept Jade, I mean Ariella, for himself. It didn't matter how much money I threw at him. He intended to keep her."

"Damnit!" I slammed my fist on the kitchen table.

Izzie was asleep upstairs, tucked into bed.

I winced. Hopefully, I didn't just wake her up.

I listened but didn't hear any noises coming from upstairs.

Good. I exhaled a heavy sigh. "I need everything on Capo Sergio. Does he live at the place this auction occurred?" We needed to know where he would take Ariella.

"No, he's got a house on a lot of land, just outside of town." Jayden paused as if he was holding his tongue, keeping something from me.

"If you know where he lives, then we go tonight." I wasn't going to wait for daylight to rescue her.

"No."

"What do you mean no?" I asked.

This had been all his fault.

Jayden didn't have to come. Hell, if he wanted to stay home and play house with Skylar or whatever, he could do that. I just needed to know where Sergio lived so that I could plan a rescue mission to retrieve Ariella.

"Sergio is sick," Jayden said and stalled for a minute.

"I don't have all day." I was growing impatient with Jayden.

"He makes what happened to the off-gridders look like a picnic."

Most of the off-gridders had been murdered in cold blood by the Russian mafia months ago. Jayden and Emma were the only two survivors, as far as I knew.

Last I heard, Emma had been hauled off in handcuffs and plead guilty to a half dozen charges.

I was surprised Jayden hadn't been behind bars with her. After all, he'd been one of the gunmen at the hostage takeover at Blue Sky Resort. Emma had been the brains behind the operation, but Jayden wasn't so innocent, either.

He had a dark past, but I was beginning to understand and unravel it because it all led back to his family, finding his niece Lexa.

"What are you suggesting?" I asked.

I valued Jayden's opinion, especially in regard to Sergio and the DeLuca family. He had far more knowledge about the mafia than I ever did. I'd done all that I could to avoid them.

"Sergio isn't going to touch your girl tonight. He always comes home after one of these parties, gets drunk, and passes out."

"And you know this because?"

Could I trust that he wouldn't lay a hand on Ariella? How confident was Jayden? I couldn't stare him in the eyes over the phone. I had to trust him, and my gut said he was honest.

"I've been invited over after a party or two," Jayden confessed. "Ariella isn't the first girl he's brought home. I should have realized that he might pick her. She's definitely his type. But I assure you, he won't touch her until tomorrow, and by the end of the week, it'll all be over."

My stomach dropped.

"Why's that?"

"He sends them on a hunt before the next auction. I've never known a girl to escape."

CHAPTER TWENTY-NINE

Jayden

I shouldn't have told Jaxson about the hunt. He'd never let me go home tonight, climb into bed, and get a few hours of shut-eye.

"You're telling me he's going to send Ariella out into what, the mountains, and hunt her down for sport?"

My mouth was dry. My eyes were blurred.

I'd already dropped Hazel off with Mason and was on my way home.

"That's right. He's a bastard, Capo Sergio, but he's never done it before fucking the hell out of the women he buys. So, you have about a week until he grows tired of the same girl and wants a new plaything."

"I can't—there's no way I can sit still and listen to this. What's the address?"

While it was a question, I knew without a doubt that Jaxson wasn't asking. He was demanding I tell him where Sergio lived.

My eyes blurred and burned. I wanted to get a few hours of sleep before the sun came up.

"You're not going alone," I said.

It was a minimum of a two-man rescue job. Someone had to kill Sergio and another rescue Ariella.

Sergio wasn't going to open his front door to Jaxson. I was the one he'd trust, the one he'd let inside his house.

Jaxson could sneak in and help Ariella escape while I distracted Sergio.

If only it were that simple.

"I don't care whether you come with me or not, but I'm not leaving Ariella there another minute," Jaxson said.

"What about your kid?" I tried throwing the Daddy card at him. It was all I had left to try to stop him from doing this tonight.

"Leave my little girl out of it!" Jaxson bellowed into the phone.

"Okay. Okay. I just meant you couldn't honestly leave a little kid like that home alone."

"She's not alone. I've got one of the guys here and Ariella's sister. Not that it's any of your concern," Jaxson spat.

Sleep was a commodity that I wasn't getting any of. Just like sex lately.

"Do you have a pen and paper? I'll give you the address. Then I need to call my house and check on Lexa."

"It's the middle of the night," Jaxson said. "Let the poor girl sleep."

Yeah. Now I understood how he felt.

I relayed the address and directions to him and then agreed to head straight there as long as he brought me a cup of coffee. I didn't care whether he brewed it at home or had a bottle of iced coffee in his fridge that he brought with him. I just needed an extra jolt of caffeine to keep me awake.

We were going on a rescue mission to get Ariella back, and I didn't want to fall asleep before my head hit the pillow.

CHAPTER THIRTY

ARIELLA

I should have been grateful the collar and bracelet were removed. Sergio may have stolen me for himself, but he didn't have any intention of sending pulse-pounding electricity through my neck.

Maybe he wasn't a sadist?

I still didn't trust him.

He'd locked me in the backseat of his black SUV, shoved a bag over my head, and drove us all of about twenty minutes.

The terrain had been rough. The ride was quite bumpy. I didn't feel like we'd stayed on any main roads.

I doubted that Sergio was concerned about being seen.

He must have lived off the beaten path. It wasn't quite off-grid, per se. I suspected there was electricity and all the finer things that money could buy.

I wasn't wrong.

"Let's go," Sergio said, his voice rough and thick. His words slurred just a bit as he grabbed me by the arm and thrust me out of the backseat.

"I can't see anything," I said, reminding him I had a bag over my head. It was difficult not to trip over the rocky terrain. He didn't have a paved driveway, or if he did, he'd opted not to use it.

"That's the point," he said.

Grass and stones grazed my bare feet.

I missed my leather boots even more, not to mention my cell phone that had been tucked away. I loved those shoes and had even splurged on them because I thought they looked fantastic with a pair of jeans.

I doubted I'd ever get them back, and breaking a new pair in was hell on my feet.

How would Jaxson ever find me?

"Step up," Sergio instructed.

I took a careful step up to feel warm wood under my toes.

Was it a porch?

It didn't creak, but it probably wasn't old or rickety, either. Sergio was a mobster and was probably rolling in dough. At least that's how I imagined it, especially after running the auction. He was clearly in charge, or else someone would have intervened when he'd decided to take me home.

I could hear the jingle of keys and the clank of metal as he shoved the key into the lock.

We would be heading inside soon.

What if I took off on foot? My hands weren't bound behind my back. I could toss off the bag over my head and run.

How far would I get?

Did he have his gun handy? I was sure he had a weapon, and he'd probably shoot me the first opportunity that he had, especially since I didn't cost him a cent.

The door squeaked on its hinge as he opened the front entrance. Well, I assumed it was the front entrance.

My heart pounded like a boat that smashed against rocks in a storm. Sweat covered me, but I knew it wasn't hot outside.

My stomach somersaulted.

At that moment, I had to act. And so I ran.

I yanked off the cloth that covered my face in my pursuit of freedom. I stumbled down the porch step, but it didn't stop me from the beginning of the chase.

I took off as fast as my legs would take me. My calves burned, but I didn't care. I refused to slow down or cower to Sergio, or any man who thought he could own me.

I was not a piece of property.

It was still dark outside, and my feet tore over the rough gravel of the thick forest.

I wished more than anything I had on my boots— something to protect the bottoms of my feet. I ran over branches and leaves, thistles, and rocks.

Everything that littered the forest floor was crunched beneath my weight as I made a beeline away from the property.

I had no idea where I was headed, only that I needed to get help.

I hadn't so much as turned around or slowed to glance back at Sergio.

He hadn't chased me, and during that brief moment, I found it strange and almost unsettling, I couldn't slow down.

I wasn't going to give him time to catch up to me if he intended to put running shoes on or change clothes. I didn't have the slightest idea why he let me run, but I wasn't going to second guess the decision.

Sure, there were bears in the woods. Grizzlies. The meanest and most deadly creatures. Possibly wolves too. I wasn't quite sure about all the wild beasts in the forest.

I hadn't lived in Breckenridge that long, and I sure didn't grow up around here.

I couldn't think about what lay beyond the forest, sleeping, or foraging for food. The only way to survive had been to escape.

Was I free?

My chest ached with a screaming intensity that made my eyes burn and tear.

Slowing down would get me killed.

I'd felt this pain before, like my chest was being crushed. Agony.

I didn't slow. I wasn't dying. It wasn't a heart attack. Sure, I had issues that made my heart quite literally skip a beat. Thanks to tachycardia and the autonomic dysfunction I was plagued with, it felt like hell.

But it wouldn't actually kill me.

Right?

I'd made sure to take my medication twice a day. I'd been religious with the routine, never missing a dose because when I did, it would tear me down, disrupting my life even the next day.

While I'd missed a dose, it wouldn't have been the end of the world if I hadn't been in fight-or-flight mode. Running for my life wasn't helping alleviate any of my symptoms.

Beyond anything, I wished I had my phone to call Jaxson.

Wincing, I remembered Delphine was coming into town tonight.

Shit.

Would she forgive me for not picking her up at the airport? We were finally reconnecting, and I'd ditched her ass.

That's what she'd say.

I could already hear her nagging tone and a look of disapproval.

Refusing to slow, I kept running through the forest. Would I reach a road, a house, some sign of civilization?

Breckenridge might have been a small town, but I'd end up there eventually, right?

What if I was headed in the wrong direction?

The world around me spun as I ran. The trees swayed, and I gripped the rough bark of one, holding myself up.

Gasping for breath, I couldn't afford to slow down.

In the distance, tires crunched on gravel.

I couldn't ascertain whether the vehicle headed toward Sergio's house or away from it. I didn't think I'd gotten turned around, but the forest seemed to extend onward forever.

Who would be coming to visit Sergio in the middle of the night?

No one.

And while I wanted to believe it was Jaxson, he probably had no idea where I was or how to find me.

Had Jayden even intended on securing my freedom, or only Hazel's? I knew there was bad blood between the two brothers, but I didn't know how bad it went.

A shotgun fired from behind, and I threw myself on the forest floor.

I hadn't heard footsteps. He'd been quiet. Unless he'd driven close by and aimed through the window of the vehicle?

I ran farther from the road, through the forest, until I ran straight into a metal fence that towered above me.

I was trapped.

CHAPTER THIRTY-ONE

JAXSON

She was out there all alone, and I was the only one who could save her.

Jayden and I pulled up outside Sergio's house. The door had been left open, the house abandoned.

While I'd expected a slew of men guarding his home like Angelo had, the fact was Sergio wasn't a mob boss. At least not yet.

I didn't know who would take Angelo's place, probably Gino, his second in command, but wars had been fought for far less amongst such men.

Jayden unholstered his gun as we quickly searched the house and the perimeter.

"They couldn't have gone far," I said. I stopped and bent down, picking up a dark cotton hood.

Jayden glanced at the material in my fist. "Think she ran?" he asked.

"Like hell I do."

Ariella was a fighter, and she'd do everything in her power to stay alive. If that meant a chance at escaping, I knew she'd take it.

I exhaled a nervous breath. I was scared for her.

She'd been through hell in a single day and was probably tired, exhausted, and I didn't even want to consider the ramifications it meant on her health.

Would she be able to run and escape?

I knew I was fit, and I'd probably be tired after being dragged around, tossed from one compound to the next, and sold at a slave auction. The trauma she'd endured alone was staggering, and thinking Sergio was still after her. To say I was worried, was an understatement.

The bastard wasn't going to give up. Not easily.

Neither would Ariella. She'd fight until the bitter end.

"We need to spread out, find her before it's too late." I unholstered my gun from my hip.

The forest extended as far as I could see, with a winding gravel road that I'd traveled in on. I hadn't spotted her cross the road, and frankly, she could be anywhere.

A shotgun rang out in the distance.

"She's got to be that way," I gestured, hearing the shotgun.

"He's hunting her, has to be," Jayden muttered under his breath.

"Or chasing her because she ran away from him."

It was as much the fact she tried to flee that resulted in Sergio hunting her down with a shotgun.

Either way, she was in danger, and I needed to find her before Sergio.

"Do you think he's got sight of her?" I didn't slow down as I popped the latch of my truck. I unzipped my tactical gear bag and retrieved a set of night vision goggles. It was the only way to find them in the dark.

While she probably hadn't been careful in her escape, examining shrubbery and broken branches would take too long. Hopefully, they hadn't gotten too far ahead.

I tossed a second pair at Jayden.

"We need to find Ariella before Sergio gets to her."

"It may be too late," Jayden said.

I wasn't accepting defeat. We'd only heard one shot. There was no scream from Ariella. No sound of victory from Sergio.

I geared up with a bulletproof vest and let Jayden help himself to any additional equipment of mine that was left over.

I grabbed a second pistol, tucking it into my boots, and a semi-automatic that I secured around my shoulder.

I wasn't taking any chances.

I jogged into the darkness, my feet not the least bit silent as my boots smashed leaves and stomped on branches.

Maybe I would get Sergio's attention and he'd leave Ariella alone.

That was my hope.

Would it go according to plan? Probably not.

At least he knew someone else was in the forest trailing him.

He wasn't alone, and neither was Ariella.

Jayden kept close behind me. It only took him a minute to catch up, and he was on my heel.

"Fan out?" he asked.

It was only the two of us.

"No. If he's got the gear, we don't want him to see both of us," I said. While I didn't want to get shot, I was also willing to die to make sure that Ariella was safe, and if that meant Jayden was getting to her in time, so be it.

I glanced down at the ground, seeing a broken branch —a sign they'd come this way through the forest.

"Keep moving," I said in a hushed whisper. The sound carried through the forest. Sound always traveled farther at night, and while I tried to keep my voice down, my feet weren't exactly quiet.

"Anything?" Jayden asked.

"Nada." I hadn't spotted any signs of life. I should have brought gear with me to detect heat signatures, but that was back at the Eagle Tactical office.

We didn't have time to call for reinforcements or request additional gear.

Ariella's life was on the line, and at any moment, Sergio could find her, shoot her, or worse, kill us and drag her back to be his sex slave.

Bile rose to my throat at the disgusting thought of what he would do to her.

My Ariella.

I'd sooner die than let him lay a hand on her.

A second shot rang out.

This time it was pointed in our direction and whizzed by, piercing a nearby tree.

The googles revealed no one to me. I held up my arm, indicating to Jayden to hold up.

Sergio had to be hiding.

Was he hidden behind a tree?

Where else could he be? I didn't see anything else, no sign of him. No sign of movement.

My eyes narrowed and twitched as I spotted the long end of the shotgun.

"Duck." I reached behind me for Jayden and threw him down on the ground with me.

Sergio had spotted us.

CHAPTER THIRTY-TWO

Jayden

Heavy footsteps pounded over the ground as Sergio rushed in our direction. Jaxson had saved my life.

Shit.

It wouldn't matter now. Any moment, he'd discover us lying on the forest floor. We had to think and move fast.

I glanced at my comrade for only a split second, and he gave off a quick nod.

He had the same idea.

We had to split up.

"I'll find her. You take care of him," Jaxson seethed.

He wasn't the least bit quiet. Did he not know how to whisper?

Did we want to give up our location to Sergio? I sure as hell didn't want him to locate us.

I took in a deep breath.

It was now or never. Jaxson had crawled away on the ground, low to the shrubs and branches, out of sight, before I spotted him leaping to his feet and running for Ariella.

Had he spotted her?

I couldn't see anything but Sergio coming right for me.

I reached for my gun, only to find the trigger jammed.

Great. Jaxson had given me a weapon that was useless.

I dropped the gun and used my fists to push the shotgun farther from me as he aimed it at my chest. I spun the weapon around, hearing the snap of his trigger finger.

Sergio dropped the gun and lunged for me. His hands fell around my neck. His grip was tight, making it hard to breathe.

I kneed him in the crotch as we rolled around on the hard surface, sticks and broken branches stabbing at us.

"You fucking bastard!" I spit as I spoke and used my thumbs to jab Sergio in the eyes.

He screamed and momentarily released his hold on my throat, long enough that I could take in a deep breath and drink in the air.

It didn't last long. He grabbed my gun that had been jammed and pulled the trigger outward, not pointing it at me.

"I'm the bastard?" he scoffed. "You come into my home and take one of my girls. Then proceed to fight me?"

Was he trying to shoot Jaxson? Had he found Ariella yet?

I couldn't see them. My focus was entirely on my own survival and stopping Sergio.

"I paid for her, fair and square." It sickened me even to think about the fact that we'd practically funded the mob by giving them money.

What other choice did we have?

At that moment, it had been the right course of action to save Hazel. If only I had been able to do the same for Ariella, we wouldn't be out here at night, wrestling for our lives.

Sergio hadn't used his dominant hand. I'd made sure to break that finger, but he held the gun in his opposite hand, continually putting pressure on the gun and trigger until it finally fired.

Shit.

Sergio's sinister laugh echoed through the forest. He rolled away from me, shooting into the darkness of night, blanketing the forest with bullet after bullet in every direction.

I could hear a high-pitched scream, female.

It had to be Ariella.

Had she been shot?

I shouldn't have ever given Sergio the opportunity to get the gun. This was my fault.

Everything was my fault. I'd caused this, and while I'd only gotten involved with Enzo and Angelo to find my niece, everyone's blood was on my hands.

I was as guilty as the mob.

CHAPTER THIRTY-THREE

ARIELLA

With my back against the metal fence, I glanced up at the barbed wire.

There was no way to scale the fence without getting hurt. I had no shoes, was wearing a scantily clad nightie, and no underwear.

It was like asking to mutilate myself.

A shot pierced through the air.

Sergio.

Maybe climbing the fence wasn't the worst idea ever.

A grumble roared in the distance.

Hell, was that a bear? No, bears didn't come out at night, right?

I had no idea if they were nocturnal. Only that I'd never seen one, minus the zoo, and I never wanted to be up close with one, either.

I skirted the fence, keeping my fingers against the metal in hopes that I'd find a break, a tear, some way to run and escape.

I tried to make myself as quiet as possible. The shotgun that had pierced through the air hadn't hit me.

Had Sergio intended it as a warning shot?

I had expected him to yell, to scream, to indicate that he wanted me to return home with him or else he'd kill me.

The silence was the only answer that followed.

I swallowed the lump that formed in my throat. Was I afraid?

Yes, I was terrified.

But I couldn't stand still.

I refused to wait to be shot or beaten, raped, or tortured by a monster.

Keeping the metal fence at my back was risky. It indicated the property line. At least I assumed that was why it existed, but it also trapped me if he drew nearer.

"Tsk. Tsk." Sergio's voice rang out in the distance.

My stomach clenched, and I froze.

Maybe he could hear my footsteps. If I didn't move, would he be unable to find me? I remained perfectly still with the calm of night.

I held my breath and listened to the sound of the wind that whipped the leaves and lapped at the trees, causing them to sway.

I, too, felt my body sway. Not from the wind, but from the exhaustion. I wanted to curl up, lie down, and sleep for a week.

My adrenaline had other ideas.

Trembling hands didn't cease to slow, but at least he couldn't hear my hands. My entire body was racked with tremors. Soon, he'd hear the rattle of the fence.

I pushed myself away from the metal.

I needed to seek shelter.

Was there a cave nearby? Perhaps a tree or large rock where I could slip away, hidden and unseen.

Did Sergio know the woods by heart? Did he frequent the area often?

This was his home, his land. I had to assume he knew every inch of the forest.

His footsteps trod away. He hurried in the opposite direction.

Where was he going? Had he given up?

I exhaled a nervous breath and kept still for another solid minute before I quietly headed toward the road. At least, that was the direction I thought I was going.

Earlier, there'd been the sound of a vehicle, traffic, which meant there were others nearby.

I needed to search whoever it was out and seek their help. Hopefully, they weren't friends with Sergio, his posse.

Time seemed to stand still. A shotgun blasted in the opposite direction.

Had Jaxson and the team come to rescue me?

I heard a scuffle in the distance. Shit.

Tears threatened my vision. I kept moving. I couldn't slow down.

I quickened my pace through the forest. My legs burned. My feet throbbed and were bloodied raw, but I didn't slow down.

What if Sergio shot whoever had come to help? What if there was no one to find me? No one to save me.

I needed to save myself.

I hurried as fast as I could. I pushed away from the fence line and kept my pace, refusing to slow down even though my feet were raw and torn with cuts and scrapes.

A hand covered my mouth.

I opened my mouth to scream and bite down on the assailant.

"Shhh, it's me, Freckles." Jaxson's warm whisper reached my ears.

I'd never been so relieved to hear that nickname or feel his body nestled tight behind me.

My body trembled, and the tears sobbed out of me like a river.

"Take a breath," Jaxson said, his voice soft and reassuring. "Jayden's with Sergio. It's not over yet."

It wasn't the time to rejoice.

Bullets flew through the air. Jaxson forced me quickly to the ground, shielding my body, lying above me, as gunfire erupted from one direction.

"Well, we know where Sergio is," Jaxson said. "I need to get you out of here and help Jayden. Can you stay down?"

"Don't leave me," I whispered. I'd never sounded so helpless in my life.

I didn't want to be helpless. I wanted to be brave, but I was afraid.

"Who else is with you?" The other members of Eagle Tactical had to be out there and could help.

"It's just Jayden and me."

I whimpered in protest. I didn't want anything to happen to him.

He unfastened his vest. "Here, put this on."

"What? No." I couldn't take it. He had a daughter at home. I had, well, I had me. That was it.

"You're wearing it. Don't argue with me," Jaxson said, his voice firm. He had already made up his mind, and I wasn't going to convince him, no matter how hard I tried.

The truth was I didn't try very hard.

I was terrified, and Sergio wanted me dead.

He probably wanted Jaxson and Jayden dead too, but those guys were former special forces. They had military training. I had nothing.

I lay cowered on the ground, and Jaxson was quick to help me secure the vest.

He was risking his life for me.

"Wait," I whispered, pulling him tight and close. My lips crashed against his.

If this was goodbye, I didn't want it to be without him knowing how I feel.

"I love you," I breathed against his lips.

Jaxson pulled back and cocked a sideways grin. "Yeah? I know. I love you too, Freckles." His lips devoured me one more time before he pulled back. "Stay here and stay down. I need to know where to find you. Don't move. No matter what. Okay?"

I nodded in understanding and watched as he took off, disappearing into the night to save Jayden and stop Sergio from killing all of us.

CHAPTER THIRTY-FOUR

JAXSON

Leaving her had been devastating, but I trusted that she'd be safe. She had my Kevlar vest, and I handed her a pistol before leaving her alone.

I wasn't going to let anything happen to Ariella ever again.

Well, at least not tonight.

I may not have been able to protect her from every little thing in the world, but I could keep her safe from Sergio and the mob.

I headed opposite the road several meters before closing in on Sergio and Jayden. I didn't want Sergio to know about my previous position.

Protecting Ariella was everything.

I hurried, not making myself too silent.

Go ahead, buddy, come at me.

He hadn't fired another shot in a few minutes, which either meant he was out of bullets or Jayden had restrained him.

There was a scuffle as I drew nearer.

Jayden and Sergio wrestled on the ground, throwing punches at one another.

That, I could handle.

With my steel-toed boots, I kicked Sergio while he was down on the ground, nailing him in the back of the neck. I grabbed him by the hair and ripped him off Jayden with one hand. My other gun was positioned at his neck.

I tilted the gun up under his chin.

"You get a kick out of abducting, selling, and raping women?"

It wasn't a rhetorical question.

He huffed and shrugged, probably trying to get out of my grasp.

I didn't let him go.

Jayden stood, dusted his pants off, and reached for the gun that was on the ground, the one that had fired several rounds at Ariella and me minutes earlier.

"Are you just going to stand there threatening or finish the job?" Jayden asked.

"Call the authorities," I said.

Jayden shook his head. "He doesn't deserve a cell and three meals a day."

"That's not up to us." I wasn't a murderer.

At least I didn't want to be one. I'd crossed the line with Angelo DeLuca. My interrogation methods had gone too far, and I had to live with what I'd done. DeLuca was a monster, same as Sergio, but killing them didn't make me the good guy.

"The hell it isn't!" Jayden lifted the gun and pointed it at Sergio's head. "Tell me why I shouldn't blast his ass to pieces?"

Sergio snickered as he stared at Jayden. "You don't have it in you."

CHAPTER THIRTY-FIVE

ARIELLA

I trembled as I lay against the grass. I'd have covered myself with branches if that had been possible.

Gunfire erupted in the distance.

My eyes slammed shut.

Silently, I prayed Jaxson was safe and that he was all right.

The Kevlar vest felt tight, constricting. I gasped for breath, finding it impossible to breathe, like I was suffocating.

Footsteps hurried through the grass in my direction.

I'd only heard one bullet.

Who'd been shot?

Was Jaxson safe?

What about Jayden?

My eyes remained shut, afraid that Sergio had survived and was gunning me down next.

Worried that he might see the whites of my eyes glinting in the moonlight, I buried my head. My hair fell around my face.

Fear didn't begin to explain the horror that flowed through my veins and pumped adrenaline to my heart.

Heavy footsteps smacked the ground.

Whoever it was didn't attempt to conceal their identity.

Why would they? It was over for them. Was it over for me?

The hurried steps came closer. "You're okay." Jaxson's voice was music to my ears, and I glanced up, making sure what I saw was real.

"I heard a gunshot." My bottom lip trembled.

Jaxson bent down and guided me to my feet. His arm stayed secure around me, his gaze glancing me over.

The adrenaline didn't cease to exist any more than it had minutes earlier. My body was racked with shivers, tremors that encompassed me from head to toe.

It wasn't a seizure. No, this was normal when the spikes of norepinephrine beat me at my own game: life.

His brow furrowed. "Jayden, give me a hand." Jaxson handed Jayden the gun that had been slung over his shoulder earlier.

Jaxson lifted me into his arms, cradling me.

"What are you doing?" I asked. I didn't fight him. I wrapped my arms around his neck as he carried me, his arms tucked under my legs.

He didn't appear to struggle in the least, but I couldn't have been easy to carry through the forest.

"You're not wearing shoes, you're visibly shaking, and I can't, in good conscience, let you walk back to the truck. It's at least a mile away," Jaxson said.

Jayden walked ahead of us a few feet. Whether he was giving us our privacy or keeping to himself, I didn't know and didn't care.

"Thank you," I whispered, exhaling a soft breath. My head leaned against his chest.

I drank in his scent, his warmth, and the comfort that he offered me.

While the tremors didn't cease, just being in his embrace was enough to bring a calmness to my emotional state, while my physical one, I still wrestled with.

"After I get you into my truck, I'm taking you to the hospital to get looked over and make sure you're all right."

Why did he have to be the sensible adult? "Jaxson," I whined. "I just want to go home."

While I knew he was looking out for my wellbeing, I didn't like hospitals.

However, I didn't know anyone who did. Even so, I would have preferred to go home, climb under the warm covers and curl up with him while I fell asleep.

"I know, and you will after you get checked out," he insisted. "Don't argue with me."

He was using that tone, the same one he used when he spoke to Izzie, and he wouldn't let her get her way.

I appreciated his protectiveness, even if I didn't want to go to the hospital. Emergency room visits were never quick. "Can't we just go to the clinic in town?" I countered.

———

Jaxson wouldn't have it. He insisted on driving me the two hours to the hospital. However, it was more like an hour and ten minutes since we were partially on the way and he drove at lightning speed.

I found it difficult to sleep. The gurney was hard and uncomfortable. The doctors had run a ridiculous number of tests.

We waited for the results.

Jaxson sat beside me, his eyelids heavy as he struggled to stay awake.

"You can shut your eyes," I mumbled.

"Not until we're home," Jaxson said.

I exhaled a heavy sigh. And when would that be? The sun was coming up already. It had been when we arrived at the hospital.

"Who's watching Izzie?" I yawned as I lay on the cot. Jaxson's hand nestled in mine.

The tremors had slowed but not fully subsided with the second bag of I.V. fluids.

We were waiting for a number of tests to come back. The doctors wanted to ensure that I wasn't drugged or facing any other issues before prescribing me my regular regimen.

"Declan's staying at the house with Izzie."

"What about Delphine? Oh my gosh, she flew in last night. I was supposed to pick her up!"

"I know," Jaxson said. He squeezed my hand gently. "She called me when she couldn't get ahold of you. I told her to take a cab and that I'd pay for the ride to my place. I also sent Declan over to let her in and put Izzie to bed. He decided to crash for the night at our place, which worked out for me."

My eyelids fluttered closed for a brief moment.

"Thank you," I whispered and opened my eyes. I struggled to stay awake. I didn't want to sleep. Not here. Not now.

"Just rest." He patted my shoulder with his other hand.

Easier said than done. The bright fluorescent overhead lights hummed with each passing second. Time felt as though it stood still. But at least I was safe.

The doctor didn't so much as knock as he pulled back the curtain and stepped into the room. "I have good news. Both of you are doing fine."

"Both of us?" What was he talking about? I glanced at Jaxson.

"Yes, you and the baby." The doctor paused. "You didn't know you were pregnant?"

"No. I mean, I didn't think I could be after the last time." I exhaled a nervous breath.

"Well, you are both healthy. However, I suggest that you see an obstetrician soon. I am concerned that one of the medications that you told us you're taking can cause issues and is not recommended to continue while pregnant. In the meantime, I'm going to give you a prescription to help lower your heart rate, but you should remain on bed rest until you see the doctor treating you for autonomic dysfunction."

"Okay," I whispered.

We were pregnant. Jaxson and I were going to have a baby.

CHAPTER THIRTY-SIX

Skylar

Jayden hadn't exactly invited me to stay with him, but I hadn't given him another option. He was the reason my brother wasn't talking to me and had kicked me out of his house.

Well, it had been a bit of my fault too, but I still needed a place to crash.

While Lincoln took Harper to get checked out, Declan eventually dropped Jayden's niece and me off at Jayden's apartment.

I was familiar with the place and gave Lexa the briefest tour before showing her the guest room.

Which meant that I was crashing in Jayden's room, whether he wanted me to or not.

I had a few things at his place already stashed away for our fake relationship arrangement. A handful of photos, some clothes, even a pillowcase on the bed, just in case his boss had shown up at the apartment to meet me unannounced.

Thankfully, that hadn't happened, although I'd dreamt of it, had nightmares of a faceless man tearing down the door and interrogating me.

And that was before I was forced to go with Angelo DeLuca and help Ben kidnap the girls.

How could I ever live with myself for what I'd done?

Would Jaxson ever forgive me? What about Ariella and Izzie?

Lexa headed straight to bed. I couldn't blame her. I was exhausted too.

I slipped into one of Jayden's t-shirts that fell just above the knee.

It smelled uniquely of him, strong and musky with a hint of sawdust. I'd never seen him work a saw, but I hadn't spent that much time with him.

I'd been angry with him, blamed him for what happened, but he went and risked his life to save Hazel and Ariella.

Maybe he wasn't the bad guy, just the bad boy.

I climbed under the covers. Everything smelled of Jayden.

The scent was overwhelming. My eyes burned as I sobbed into the pillow.

I hated myself, what I'd done, what I'd become to save myself.

How would I make it up to my family, my friends?

It was impossible to sleep. I tossed and turned. Without my phone, I didn't have the slightest idea when Jayden would come home or if he'd come home alive.

What if the auction took a turn for the worse?

The night dragged on, and daylight finally shined through the curtains. Just as I started to drift to sleep from exhaustion, the bedroom door opened, and I was startled awake.

"Jayden?" I mumbled and rubbed the sleep from my eyes.

"It's all over," he said, his voice rough and thick.

"Hazel and Ariella, are they okay?" I asked as I sat up in bed. I pulled the surrounding covers tight into my fists.

"Hazel, I rescued from the auction. Jaxson and I had to go after Capo Sergio and retrieve Ariella. She's on the way to the hospital, but I think she's all right." He stripped down, not seeming to care that I was in his bed.

His shoes were first left on the floor as he removed his shirt and tossed it into the nearby hamper. Jayden unzipped his pants and tossed those in the bin along with his boxers.

I tried not to stare.

He didn't seem to care in the least. He stalked across the room for the bathroom and flipped on the light.

My eyes burned, and I squinted as he left the door open. "I'm going to shower. I need to rid myself of all this filth. Did you get washed up already?" Jayden asked.

"I uh, no." I had been too tired, too broken to do anything but wallow in self-pity. "I probably should have."

"You want to get cleaned up with me? Share a shower? Conserve water together."

I rubbed my tired eyes and shifted on the mattress, tossing my legs over the side. I swayed for a second before stepping forward, following him into the bathroom.

"That's my girl," Jayden said and quirked a sideways grin. "I'm so sorry about what happened."

"Shhh," I said, silencing him with my finger to his lips.

He kicked the door shut with his foot and backed me up against it, bringing my hands up above my head.

"I've wanted to do this with you since you first walked into the bar," Jayden whispered.

He didn't kiss me. Just stared at me. Was he teasing me on purpose?

"What are you waiting for?" I asked, trying to catch my breath.

"Permission," Jayden said, his voice raspy and low. "Unlike those men, I won't take what isn't mine."

"I want to be yours," I confessed.

Was that what he wanted to hear?

His lips descended hard on mine, our mouths crashing together, tongues dueling for control.

He kept me pinned to the door, his body pressed tight, naked.

The only thing between us was the shirt that I wore.

"You're going to have to take this off if you plan on showering," Jayden said, eyeing my shirt.

I chuckled, my arms still pinned against the door above my head.

"Kind of hard to do without the use of my arms. Maybe you should undress me," I said.

Jayden growled. His desire poked at me. He moved my hands together, one hand holding me firm, the other guiding my shirt inch by inch up. His touch was warm and gentle, far more tender than I had anticipated.

His lips teased my ear, sending a shudder through my body as I grew antsy with need.

"I'm so sorry," he whispered into my ear. Soft kisses danced over my neck as he dropped his tight hold on my wrists, freeing me. "I shouldn't have risked your life." His eyes bore into mine.

"We both made mistakes," I admitted, meeting his stare. We would have to live with those consequences. Right now, I just needed to feel alive and loved.

I leaned forward, and our lips collided once again. I didn't want to hear his apologies. I wanted to feel his admiration and his care.

"I need to forget," I whispered against his lips and gently tugged on his bottom lip with my teeth. "Please, make the pain go away."

Jayden opened his mouth and expelled a soft sigh. Was he going to tell me that he didn't know how?

As quickly as the look of darkness and sadness crossed his face, it was gone.

His mouth descended onto mine, and he removed the last barrier between us, tossing the shirt to the floor. Jayden scooped me up into his arms and put me down to sit at the edge of the bathroom sink.

He retrieved a condom from the drawer, ripped it open, and unraveled it before his gaze met mine.

"Are you sure?"

"Yes," I said. My hand reached for him, stroking him, touching him, proving to him that I wanted this with him.

I'd been through hell today, but the other girls, the ones who were supposed to be my friends, had been through so much worse. Jayden didn't have to tell me what he'd witnessed to see the pain and anguish behind that steel gaze.

His warmth filled me, fueled me, and made me forget the pain and ache that had been darkening my heart.

I wrapped my legs around him and pulled him deeper and tighter with each thrust. My fingers dug into his shoulder, marking him.

Jayden grunted and he pulled out, running a hand through his hair. His eyes looked distraught.

"Are you seriously going to tease me to death?" Why the hell had he stopped?

"This was not how I wanted our first time to be," he rasped, meeting my stare. "You deserve better."

"I'm not sure about that." I laughed darkly. I stared at him, my gaze unwavering. My fingers trailed a delicate path down his chest. "Please, I just want to feel something other than regret, and with you, I could never regret this."

Jayden's lips came down hard on mine. "I've imagined fucking you in the bar for the past several months," he whispered. "But you deserve the royal treatment. Wine, dinner, and lots of foreplay."

"That sounds nice for next time. Tonight, I don't care that it's in the bathroom or if it were in the bar. I just want to listen to you moan and hear you scream my name."

"Bossy." Jayden laughed. His fingers tangled in my hair as he brought my lips down to his, clinging to me, our kisses fiery and feisty as he entered me again.

I moaned in pleasure. I wanted him to know that he made me feel good, and I didn't want him to have any further second thoughts.

There would be no regrets tonight, at least not between the two of us.

My eyes slammed shut as the sensation grew, building and intensifying.

"Come for me, Skylar," he whispered into my ear.

I tightened around him, my insides pulsating. Already, I was so close, teetering on edge. My toes curled, and I listened as he grew near.

Everything felt like fireworks exploding around me as I trembled in his embrace, gasping for breath as we both came undone.

"Shower?" he mumbled as he slid out and tossed the condom into the trash.

I laughed under my breath. That was why I'd joined him in the bathroom. I slid off the counter, my legs like jelly.

Jayden steadied me, his hands on my hips. "Are you okay?"

I nodded, staring up at him. "Perfect."

CHAPTER THIRTY-SEVEN

ARIELLA

I'd fallen asleep in the truck on the way home from the hospital.

I didn't know how Jaxson had managed to stay awake.

The truck pulled to a soft halt, but it stirred me awake. "We home?" I yawned and rubbed the sleep from my eyes.

"Yes," Jaxson said. He shut off the engine and climbed out, coming around to help me out and carry me through the front door.

My feet were bandaged and sore as hell from the chase through the forest, but I would survive. Besides, that was the least of my worries.

I was pregnant, and not only did I have to look after myself, now I had to think about the little boy or girl growing inside of me.

Crippling fear was an understatement of how I felt.

Jaxson carried me inside, sat me down on the sofa and shut off the alarm before he locked the house up. "Do you want to head right to bed, or are you hungry?"

I could barely keep my eyes open. "Sleep sounds wonderful. I can just crash on the couch." I shifted to stretch out.

"Izzie will be up soon," Jaxson reminded me. "How about I take you up to bed and tuck you in?"

"What about you?" I didn't want to be away from him. I knew it was probably a combination of the hormones and the trauma of what I'd been through, but I was feeling incredibly needy.

I hated the way I felt, like I didn't want ever to be alone again.

"I'm exhausted. I'll climb into bed as soon as I let Declan know we're home. Okay?"

————

"You're home," Delphine said, a warm smile on her face. "I'm glad you're okay. Your boyfriend's friend told me what happened. Declan, is it?"

My boyfriend.

I smiled faintly at my sister calling Jaxson that term. We hadn't used labels.

"Yeah, sorry I missed you at the airport."

Delphine waved her hand dismissively. "It's not a big deal. I mean, with what you went through, don't even think about it." She scooted closer to me on the sofa. "Is it true that Ben was behind your abduction?"

I exhaled a heavy sigh. I wasn't sure I was ready to talk about it, but it seemed Declan had looped her in on what he knew at the time.

I didn't blame him. He had to tell her something, and it was better she knew the truth.

At least then she wouldn't hate me for not showing up when I promised to give her a ride.

"It's okay if you don't want to talk about it," Delphine said. She stood and headed to the kitchen. "I'm going to grab myself a cup of coffee. Do you want some?"

"I can't," I said. I had to watch everything that elevated my heart rate, even more so with the pregnancy.

"Oh, that's right." Delphine assumed it had been because of my health condition. She'd been blessed with great genes.

Not me.

We still hadn't told anyone about the baby. I didn't want to jinx it.

"I'm glad you flew here. It's good to see you," I said. Things still felt strained, but at least she was trying. I felt like I'd been the only one trying since Ben's initial arrest over a year ago.

Delphine wrapped an arm around me, giving me a much-needed and long-awaited hug. "Sis, there is nowhere else I'd rather be. I'm sorry I listened to my stupid husband. I should have ditched his ass and flown out here sooner."

I laughed under my breath. "It's all right. Love makes us do stupid things."

"Tell me about it," Delphine said with a grin.

"What made you decide to come out here now, after all this time?" I asked. It couldn't just be that she realized Ben was a jerk.

Delphine's smile faded from her lips. "The truth is that your boyfriend called me."

"What?" My stomach sank.

Why would Jaxson do that?

"He called to tell me about how, a few months ago, you'd been kidnapped by Ben, and he asked me to come and see you. I should have come sooner."

I wanted to be angry with Jaxson for interfering, but I understood what he was doing. His intentions were good, but I wasn't happy about him going behind my back.

"I can't believe he called you," I said.

"He wouldn't have had to call me if you'd told me that Ben had abducted you," Delphine said. "I just wish that you trusted me. We're family, and I know that I haven't always been there for you. I'm sorry."

"It's in the past." I wanted to forgive her and move on. She was here now, and that was what mattered, right?

We were finally reconnecting.

"Is Ben in prison again?" Delphine asked. "Did they catch him? Declan was explaining that Ben had been part of the human trafficking ring."

"Jaxson and the team are tracking him down as we speak."

Her brow creased. "They'll catch him, right?"

I'd never feel safe until he was arrested and behind bars.

CHAPTER THIRTY-EIGHT

Jayden

I wasn't thrilled with being back here without a weapon.

Jaxson had insisted I wear an earpiece and a wire that relayed everything I said to the Eagle Tactical team.

They wanted to nail Enzo Ricci and, more importantly, find Benjamin Ryan.

Stalking up to the front door of Enzo's luxurious mansion, I stood in front of the door, palm raised.

I gave a firm knock and waited.

Silence was the only response I received.

"Don Ricci?" I knocked again and rang the doorbell.

Still no answer.

I stepped off the porch and glanced through the window. The lights were off. There was no sign of anyone inside.

Three cars were parked in front of the property, but the car I knew he drove regularly, the electric blue Evora Lotus, was nowhere in sight.

"He's not here," I said to Jaxson and the team.

They had sent me on a mission but weren't far, listening to the wire from their truck. They were on standby, should I require backup.

"You have other connections to the Ricci family. Call them." Jaxson's tone was firm and sent a shudder down my spine.

"Yeah, on it."

I exhaled a heavy sigh and dug my cell phone from my pocket. I scrolled through my phone and stopped when I landed on Dante Ricci's name.

He was Enzo's second.

We'd done business together, and he'd been the one to inform me what had been going on when Enzo had tossed me out of the party and taken possession of Skylar.

My blood was boiling just thinking about the way they'd treated her and me, like pawns.

Dante picked up on the first ring.

"Didn't expect to hear from you," Dante said.

"I need to see you." I didn't want to do this over the phone.

I waited for a beat. Silence filled the phone line.

"Dante?"

Had he hung up?

"I'll come to the bar," Dante said. "Twenty minutes."

It would take me twenty-five to get to the bar where I worked. I hung up the call and hurried toward my vehicle.

"Dante is having me meet him at the bar," I said. There was only one bar in Breckenridge.

"We're heading there now," Lincoln responded into the communication device.

"Great," I muttered. That's just what I needed, the entire Eagle Tactical team and the mafia coming head-to-head.

My foot was like lead on the pedal, flying through the gravel roads, kicking up stones and dirt in a cloud of dust behind me.

I hurried toward the bar. I shouldn't have been surprised that Dante wanted to meet me there. It was, after all, their turf.

Dante owned the bar, laundered money through it, and that had been how he'd gained power with Enzo, earning his trust as his second.

What happened to Enzo?

Was he at the bar with Dante right now? Had that been why they'd asked me to join them?

I pulled up out front and shut off the engine. Exhaling a heavy breath, I checked the glove compartment for a weapon.

I shoved the Glock into the waistband of my pants before I stepped out and headed for the front door of the bar.

The hinges on the heavy wood squeaked as I yanked it open.

In the corner booth, the darkest part of the bar, Dante sat his back to the wall, his gaze on the door.

Jaxson and Lincoln sat at the bar, both of them with a drink in their hands, but they didn't appear to be throwing any back.

The place was mostly empty.

Dante had been waiting for me.

How long had he been here?

Dante nursed a cold bottle of beer. His fingers stroked the glass. "Nice of you to join me," he said.

I climbed into the booth and sat opposite of him. I wasn't comfortable with my back to the door. My stomach sunk from the feeling that someone could come up from behind and I wouldn't see them.

But Jaxson and Lincoln were a few feet away. They'd have my back.

At least I hoped they'd have my back. I hadn't exactly had theirs lately.

I was trying to make amends and do right by them.

"Enzo didn't answer his door," I said.

Dante shrugged and sipped his beer. "I suppose he's not home."

Well, that was cryptic.

"I have questions," I said. "For starters, you all betrayed me, snatching my fiancée and handing her over to the enemy."

Dante held up a hand. "Was she really your fiancée?"

Had he seen through the charade?

"Where's Benjamin Ryan?" I asked, ignoring Dante's question and changing the subject.

"You mean the rat," Dante muttered under his breath. "You tell me. You hired him." Dante's eyes tightened and flinched.

"You know where he is," I said and leaned forward. "Tell me, and I'll keep you out of this mess that Enzo and Angelo dug for themselves."

He took another swig of his beer. "They dug their graves. I always told Enzo not to deal with Angelo. You can't ever trust another don, but Enzo was all brass and no brains."

Was?

Did he realize that he spoke about him in the past tense?

"Enzo's dead?" I asked.

Dante didn't answer my question. At least not directly.

"He made his bed and is lying in it."

"What about Ben?" I asked. "He betrayed the Ricci Family. That doesn't come without a cost."

Dante finished his beer and gestured the bartender over for a second. He waited until we were alone again before speaking.

"Do you know that Enzo suspected that you were the traitor?" Dante asked.

I held my tongue, not wanting to reveal that Enzo was right. I had betrayed him to save those girls, but

I hadn't been the only one. Ben had betrayed all of us.

"If I was, would I be coming to you?" I asked. "Seems like suicide."

"Truth is I never liked Enzo's recent business dealings." He huffed and shook his head. His top lip snarled with disgust. "I'm no saint by any means, but things are going to start cleaning up around here, and you can guarantee that DeLuca's men will be driven out of town."

Was that a threat?

"You're the new don," I said, letting the realization dawn on me that Dante had taken over the Ricci Family. Not only was he second, but he also had Enzo's men behind him, an army that supported him.

"You're lucky I like you," Dante said. "But I don't trust you to be an associate anymore. That was Enzo who wanted to hire you. You can come and have a drink on me, but you need to find another place of employment."

That was fine with me.

"We're not going to let you steal any more women or children." I wanted it made clear that I wasn't going to allow him to hurt anyone else in Breckenridge.

Dante laughed under his breath. "As I stated earlier, I wasn't a fan of Enzo's business practices and have no intention of continuing his games. I have other matters that have captured my interest that I don't care to discuss with you."

He took another swig from his beer before putting the bottle down forcefully against the table. "Your fiancée, or whatever she is, I have no desire for her. As long as she keeps my name out of her mouth, you can rest assured that my men will leave you alone."

"Is that a threat?" If Skylar testified against Dante, was he going to endanger her life?

Dante smiled. "The way I see it, I've done nothing wrong. Enzo snatched your fiancée, and you hired Ben. My hands are clean."

"Where is Ben?" I'd come here to locate Benjamin Ryan, and I hadn't gotten the slightest detail on where to track him down.

"You tell me; he betrayed the Ricci Family for the DeLuca Family. Rats end up dead, but I didn't kill him. He wasn't massacred in the bloodshed?"

I opened my mouth but shut it just as quickly. Ben was dirty, but I wasn't a saint, either. How I'd managed to avoid jail and turn my life around was a miracle.

"If I get my hands on Ben, he's a dead man. Then again, maybe I should thank him. With Don DeLuca out of the picture, Sergio dead, and his guards mopped all over the compound, my newest enemy is Angelo's second, Gino, and he's too old to be on the front lines. It's like being don was just handed to me. And in a matter of time, the DeLucas will be under my control. I'm guessing I have you and your pretty little team to thank for that?"

Dante held up a beer to say 'cheers' to Jaxson and Lincoln as they sat at the bar.

"The best part is I've got my sights on Gino's daughter, Nicole. That hot little piece of ass, I'm going to get my hands on her and ruin her."

CHAPTER THIRTY-NINE

ARIELLA

I still couldn't believe the doctor at the hospital. He had to have been wrong.

Pregnant?

How was I pregnant? I mean, yes, we hadn't been one hundred percent careful, but I was assured that I couldn't get pregnant again.

My last, and only, pregnancy with my son had been difficult. He'd been born early and hadn't survived life outside of N.I.C.U.

Worry filled every ounce of me, and while Jaxson had accompanied me to an obstetrician, neurologist, and midwife, they all confirmed that I was doing well, had adjusted the medication I was on, and assured me that the baby was in good health according to every test they'd run.

Bed rest wasn't a requirement as long as I was taking it easy, not undergoing too much stress, and my heart rate was within the normal perimeters.

The doctors also assured Jaxson and me that we could have sex, as long as we were careful not to do anything too strenuous, and recommended a bed, anything to keep me seated or lying down.

My cheeks had flamed with embarrassment. But Jaxson had seemed like he was mentally taking notes at the appointments, learning what he could and couldn't do with his pregnant girlfriend.

Jaxson insisted I monitor my heart rate constantly, which wasn't complicated with a smartwatch. He was more than just a tad overprotective, but I appreciated his concern.

Besides, he wasn't the only one worried about the health of the baby.

How could I not have fears after the last time I'd been pregnant? The good news was that the chronic symptoms that plagued me were minimal in my second trimester. Being pregnant had at least temporarily made me feel better.

I could get around easier without my heart rate skyrocketing when I stood. My stomach, while in knots, had been over concern for our little one and not from the adrenaline spikes that I had been accustomed to.

As we curled up in bed together, Jaxson's hand grazed my growing belly. While I hadn't felt our little pumpkin yet, it was only a matter of time.

I rolled onto my back, and Jaxson lifted the hem of my shirt, dropping soft kisses over my belly. "I've never seen you so eager to kiss my stomach," I teased.

His long, dark lashes fluttered as he smiled up at me. "I will have to rectify that, Freckles." His touch was soft and light and made my stomach feel like a thousand butterflies.

My eyes widened, realizing it wasn't my nerves or his touch exciting me. Well, it did that too. But it was the baby.

"Oh my gosh! Did you feel that?" I asked, staring into Jaxson's gaze.

"The baby likes my attention."

"What sane person wouldn't?" I asked. My fingers tangled in Jaxson's hair, caressing his scalp. "I'm almost afraid to admit it, but I like being pregnant."

Jaxson stared up at me. His breath hovered against my stomach. His hand rested over the small bump. "It suits you," he said. "The saying is true that a pregnant woman glows."

I rolled my eyes and scrunched my nose. "I'm not sure I believe that," I said, laughing. "But you should know, my symptoms that I'm accustomed to—the heart rate issues, nausea, all the chronic bad stuff, seem better. Like being pregnant healed me. I mean, it's probably crazy and nonsense, but if I always felt this good, I'd be happy always to be pregnant."

He quirked a grin. "So, we're going to have a herd of little Monroes running around here?"

I smacked his arm. "They're not cattle!" Shaking my head, laughing, it felt good not to have to hide our relationship or the fact that he was the father of my little pumpkin.

"Platoon?" he grinned. "I can have my own little Eagle Tactical army."

"You are horrible!" I pointed my finger at him. "You're not teaching our boys or girls any military training. They're children."

Jaxson leaned in and planted a soft kiss on my forehead. "I know that. I meant when they're older. Not just boys, but grown men. So, like when they're thirteen."

"Oh, brother," I muttered.

His fingers tickled my hips as he inched my shirt higher, disrobing me of my clothes.

"Another added benefit." He grinned, admiring my round breasts. "I could get used to keeping you pregnant and barefoot in the kitchen."

"You'd better be teasing!" I swatted at him, and he grabbed my wrist and pinned me down on the mattress.

"Maybe we should try to make another brother or sister," Jaxson teased.

I rolled my eyes. "You know it doesn't work like that. You can't get a pregnant woman knocked up."

"Really?" He quirked his head to the side with a laugh. "Are you sure? I think we need to test that theory."

His breath teased my lips apart. I wanted more. His fingers were caressing me, undressing my pajama shorts and panties.

"When did you become a scientist?" I joked, continuing our playful banter. For the first time in a long time, I felt free, safe, and unconditionally loved.

My fingers pushed at his boxers. I tugged them down his hips and felt the bed shift as he kicked the cotton material to the floor. "Didn't you get the memo? The boys at Eagle Tactical and I are all—"

"Stop right there." I held up a hand. "I don't know where this is going, but you're the only one testing that theory with me."

Jaxson grinned. His cheeks reddened. "That's not what I was suggesting!"

"Good, because I want only one man for the rest of my life." The confession spilled out before I'd even realized what I'd said.

He felt that way too about me, right?

"Good, because that's exactly what I want. You and Izzie. The two girls who vie for my attention."

"Yeah, well, that's totally different. Izzie can have your attention." The grin spread across my face as my fingers trailed soft, featherlight touches over his chest and down toward what I had my sights on. "I get your body."

"So that's all I'm worth to you, sex?" Jaxson asked. He laughed, not sounding the least bit upset or mad.

"Well, that's not all you're worth. Your mind is sexy too." I grinned up at him. "Come here and kiss me already."

His lips descended on mine, his breath warm and comforting, his body making my insides ache with his soft caress and gentle kisses. He was an expert in making me restless and full of need.

We rolled around in bed, each of us vying for control. Warm, strong hands caressed every inch of my skin, setting me ablaze.

I couldn't take much more of his teasing. My hand moved down to stroke him, touch him, and guide him inside my warmth.

I needed him like I needed air to breathe. "Please," I whispered, wanting this dance between us to quicken.

I'd never felt quite so desperate in my life, desiring something so much that I thought I might die if I didn't have it.

His eyes were bright and wide. His mouth covered mine as I moaned.

We had to be quiet.

Izzie was in bed, and we definitely did not want to wake her.

His warmth filled me, and his hands clasped mine as he slowly began moving, savoring each moment together.

"God, you're going to kill me," I muttered.

Sweat coated my skin.

My heart pounded against my chest, but it felt good.

Satisfying.

"More," I grunted.

Maybe it was the hormones and the fact that I was pregnant, but I couldn't seem to get enough of Jaxson. My fingernails grazed over his back and down to his bottom, pulling him tighter, claiming him for me.

His pace quickened, sensing my urgency and need.

Everything inside of me ached.

My heated core trembled and throbbed as he filled me, fueled me, and satisfied me.

Toes curled, I clung to him with eyes closed as fireworks danced over my vision. Gasping for breath, panting hard and held him tight as he came undone with me.

He was quick to roll off and pull me against him. "I don't want to squish you or hurt the baby."

"You won't," I said with a soft laugh. "Our little pumpkin is well protected." I gently patted the slight bulge of my stomach.

Curled against Jaxson, my fingers danced in his hair, my eyes never leaving his. "Your sister, Skylar, wants to throw me a baby shower. Well, us."

"No."

"Come on. She's trying to make amends," I said.

His eyes twitched. "What she did, it's unforgivable."

He was one stubborn man. I'd give him that. "Yes, but she's trying to do better. She's your sister. Didn't you forgive Jayden?" I asked.

"That's different."

Jaxson had offered Jayden a spot with the Eagle Tactical team. I'd been surprised that he'd invited him to join them and even more shocked to learn that Jayden had accepted the offer.

"How?" I asked.

"I expected Jayden to betray me."

I sat up slightly in bed. My fingers paused in his hair. "You are so full of shit." I grabbed the pillow and smacked him playfully with it.

"You did not just hit me with a pillow."

"Oh, I did," I countered. "And you can't hit your pregnant wi—girlfriend back."

Jaxson grabbed me by the hips and tucked me under him, straddling me. His hands tickled my hips. "That's not what you were going to say."

I kept my mouth shut. My eyes were wide, and I was trying desperately not to laugh too loud and wake Izzie next door.

"You don't know what I was going to say," I countered.

Jaxson's hands stalled on my hips. "Is that so? It sounded quite a bit like you were about to refer to yourself as my pregnant wife."

His gaze bored into mine.

Shit.

He went there.

He said what I was desperately trying not to say and that had slipped out inadvertently. It just felt natural, far more familiar, and better than when I'd been married the first time around.

I had sworn I'd never remarry. And I'd meant it until I met Jaxson.

We were having a pumpkin together.

I could still hear Jaxson's voice in my head. The first words he'd said when I'd referred to the baby as pumpkin. *You've got to be kidding me!* He'd come to understand it was a coping mechanism and a way to discuss the baby without me fretting that I'd jinx it.

He'd gone along with it because he was Jaxson Monroe, and he'd do anything for those he loved.

"Well?" Jaxson smiled. He stared down at me, waiting for my answer.

"I didn't hear you propose," I countered.

Two could play at that game.

"I'm not going to."

The smile fell from my face.

Wow. He went there.

I tried to slip from his embrace, but he wouldn't let me.

Tears threatened my vision. The room felt hot, stuffy. "Let me up," I gasped. I needed to move, get out of bed, run to the bathroom.

And do what?

Cry?

Hide?

I felt like a fool.

"Ariella, look at me."

My bottom lip trembled, and he guided my chin to meet his stare.

"I'm not going to propose to you until I know you'll say yes."

"What?" Had I heard him correctly?

I blinked back the tears. Now I felt like a mess. An even bigger one that I had moments earlier when I thought he said he'd never want to marry me.

"I want it to be a big, fancy ordeal, and I'm not going to have you blow my ego and say no." Jaxson grinned as he stared down at me.

I wiped the single tear that had fallen down my face.

I was a mess. A pregnant, hormonal mess. Which was Jaxson's fault. But even so, he'd been sweet and kind, and I'd jumped to conclusions.

"I'll marry you on one condition," I said, staring up at him through glistening eyes.

He stared and waited for me to continue.

"You make amends with Skylar."

Jaxson whined like a child as he straddled my hips. "Aww, come on. After what she did to you and Izzie? How am I supposed to forgive her?"

"She's trying. Maybe baby steps," I said. "She's your family, and I know she was selfish and put all of our lives at stake, but I've come to forgive her."

"Really? You don't hate her in the slightest bit?" Jaxson asked.

I wasn't going to lie to him. "Oh, I'm still mad at her, but I'm working through my anger. You've forgiven Jayden. It's time for you to make amends with Skylar."

He exhaled loudly through his nose. "I don't know, Freckles. You're asking an awful lot of me."

I laughed at the absurdity of the situation. "And marrying you will be a picnic?" I grinned up at him.

"Damn right, it will be. I'll be your knight in shining armor," Jaxson said. "I'll sweep you off your feet and carry you over the threshold."

"Yeah, right, before knocking my head into a wall. I've seen the movies. No thanks."

Jaxson leaned down. His lips grazed mine. "How about I think about it?"

"What? Marrying me?"

"No, silly. Forgiving Skylar," Jaxson said. "I definitely want to marry you."

"Good, because she's hosting the baby shower. She'll be over next Saturday. You can work things out with her."

A part of me still hated Skylar for what she'd done, but I understood she'd been coerced into helping Ben, or Angelo DeLuca would have sold her as part of the slave auction. Her life depended on it, and while she hadn't intended to kidnap anyone but me, hoping that I would be able to save the two of us, her plan had imploded.

At least that's the story she gave me when we sat at the coffee shop to talk.

"Fine, but if she so much as looks at you the wrong way, she's gone," Jaxson said.

"Good." I leaned over and planted my lips on his. "I'd expect nothing less from the man I love."

EPILOGUE

JAXSON

Everything had fallen into place. Ariella had delivered a healthy baby girl whom we named Olivia Monroe.

Izzie had been ecstatic to have a baby sister but hadn't quite understood why she couldn't play tea party or push her on the swings just yet.

Harper had been blessed with a surprise, twins. The doctors had been shocked to discover in the third trimester that there had been a second baby, a boy hiding behind his sister.

Harper was thrilled by the news.

Lincoln hid his initial panic well, and by the time the twins were born, they handled it together like a pro.

It also helped that Harper still had residual royalties from her film career, and they could afford to hire a nanny to help out with the twins.

A firm knock echoed through the front door.

"Just a second!" I called out, holding little Olivia in my arms. She was cuter than any pumpkin that I'd ever laid eyes on.

I glanced through the peephole, surprised to see Sheriff Nelson on the opposite side.

I turned off the alarm and unlocked the front door, greeting him. "Sheriff, I didn't expect to see you," I said.

"I wanted to bring you the news in person."

It had better be good news. I couldn't handle anything terrible. "Yes?" I asked. My mouth was dry, parched.

"Is this your little one?" Sheriff Nelson asked, cooing at Olivia.

"Sure is. Sheriff Nelson, please tell me it's good news that you have."

"It is." He nodded firmly. "We tracked down Ben Ryan last night. We received a tip from an anonymous source and discovered him nailed to a wall with his own nail gun."

I did my best to look surprised.

"Wow."

I hadn't told Ariella that the boys and I had located Ben last night, played with him a bit, and then called in the local police to make sure that he survived to stand trial.

"You don't look that surprised," Sheriff Nelson said.

"No, I am. I'm relieved that it will finally be over." I bounced Olivia as she started fussing in my arms.

Had my newborn daughter sensed my frustration and anger with Ben? I hadn't wanted to worry Ariella; it had been why I hadn't told her that we'd tracked him down to a shed that he was living in, next door to us.

He'd taken up residence in the shed on her old property.

Had he been stalking us?

Waiting for the moment to snatch our children or hurt my fiancée? I refused to stand still and wait for him to ruin our lives, again.

"He's been arrested and charged with kidnapping, child endangerment, attempted murder, trafficking women across state lines, the list goes on," the sheriff said.

"I'm just glad you guys finally nailed the guy."

The sheriff's eyebrow twitched. "I really hope you weren't involved, Monroe."

"I'm sure you asked Ben and he told you the truth."

Sheriff Nelson rolled his eyes. "Like they always do. Anyway, I've already spoken with Skylar Monroe, Hazel Agron, and Harper Madison. They've all agreed to testify against Benjamin Ryan. Your wife, Ariella Monroe, was kidnapped twice by Ben. Her testimony would go a long way to help keep him locked up indefinitely."

"I'll do it," Ariella said as she came around the corner from the hallway into the living room.

I hadn't heard her sneak in.

Shit.

Had she heard how he'd been found, nailed to the wall?

"Are you sure?" I glanced back at Ariella.

"Yes, I need to make sure that he never sees a day outside of prison again."

I'd be there for Ariella every step of the way. "Okay. What about Enzo Ricci?" I asked the sheriff. "Has there been any word about him?"

While I'd had to give a statement along with the Eagle Tactical guys about Angelo and Sergio DeLuca, Enzo had been involved. He'd handed my sister over to Angelo without her consent and triggered this train wreck of circumstances.

"He's gone. Missing, as far as we can tell. Left town, and no one's seen or heard from him. At least no one's talking. We suspect foul play. It's possible one of DeLuca's men crossed him and killed him, but we've recovered no body, and there's been no apparent crime scene."

"He's still out there," Ariella said. She folded her arms across his chest.

"I wouldn't lose any sleep over it. He knows the local sheriff and the feds are looking for him. If he's smart, he left town, flown to another country that doesn't have extradition. The feds flagged his passport, but a guy like him, he doesn't fly commercial."

Based on the conversation Jayden had with Dante, I suspected Enzo was dead.

The mafia knew how to cover up and destroy evidence.

No one would find Enzo, ever.

"And the human trafficking ring?" I asked. We'd handed over the information that we had obtained, and the eyewitness testimony from Ariella, Hazel, and Jayden was enough to put the DeLuca Family out of business.

Dante Ricci was still out there, but he'd sworn that he'd taken his business ventures in a different direction.

Olivia began fussing, and Ariella stepped in, taking her from my arms to feed her.

"No more shipments are coming in and out of Breckenridge. We've got feds keeping a watch on

Gino DeLuca and Dante Ricci. If either of them so much as slips up and they will, just give it time, we'll be on their asses."

"Thank you," I said, relieved to hear that it finally would all behind us.

The mafia probably still laundered money, sold drugs or weapons, but at least it wasn't people.

I walked the sheriff out and secured the door behind him, turning the alarm back on. You could never be too safe.

"Are you sure you want to testify against Ben?" I asked.

Ariella sat on the sofa feeding our baby girl who was cradled in her arms.

"I don't see another choice. I need to keep my family safe, and the best way to do that is to lock that bastard behind bars."

Izzie jumped down the steps, two at a time, hopping like a kangaroo before hurrying over to sit next to her baby sister.

"Momma, what's a bastard?" Izzie asked.

Shit.

Some things never changed.

————

Thank you for reading Covert: Jayden. I hope you've enjoyed the entire Eagle Tactical series.

Want to see more of Dante and the Ricci Family?

Secret Vow, the first book in the Mafia Marriages series, is hotter and darker, but each book will deliver a happily ever after!

There will even be a special appearance from one of the main characters in the Eagle Tactical series. But don't worry, I promise not to destroy their happy ending.

She wants her freedom, and all I want is her...

Nicole DeLuca, she's the daughter of the biggest crime boss on the west coast. Did I mention that her father, Gino DeLuca, is my enemy?

I slept with Nikki, and I can't for the life of me forget about her. I've been keeping tabs on her, making sure no other men come anywhere near her.

I'll chase them away like the beast that I am to protect her.

Like a caged bird, she's desperate for freedom. Nikki sneaks out only to get snatched and sold as a bride.

Even in the darkest room, the dirtiest corner of the world, I recognize her. She's my little dove.

I buy her. Own her. Save her.

Except she doesn't see it that way...

She wants her freedom, and all I want is her and that baby.

One-click Secret Vow now!

———

Sign up for Willow Fox's newsletter

And I'm thrilled to offer a sneak peek of BRUTAL BOSS, a spicy dark bratva romance with a happily ever after.

———

Standing outside Steele Concierge Medical, I stare up at the tall, white building as it towers above me. I feel small and insignificant in comparison, but my contribution is more than just as a nurse.

"Waiting for something?" Hannah asks.

I take a swig from the cup of coffee in my hand. "The caffeine to kick in?" I was waiting for my colleague with the FBI, Special Agent Savannah Blakely, to make contact. She never did show up at the coffee shop.

Hannah grabs my arm and drags me in through the front door, oblivious to the fact that I secretly work for the FBI as a forensic nurse.

We show our badges to security before being granted entrance past the lobby for the elevators.

"Check out the eye candy at six o'clock," Hannah whispers to me as we approach the long hallway of elevators. There are eight elevators, four on each side, making it so that no one has to wait too long for a ride up to their floor.

I suppose when you pay twenty-five thousand dollars a person per yearly enrollment fee, the least they can do is not make it a long wait to see your physician.

I inconspicuously glance in the direction Hannah suggests. A gentleman with a dark, scruffy beard, dark eyes, and tattoos covering his arms, chest, and up to his neck meets my stare.

It's Mikhail Barinov, my target.

Is that why Savannah bailed on my ass this morning? Did she see him enter the building on her way to the coffee shop?

I wouldn't expect a text or phone call from her. My FBI-issued cell phone is at my desk in the city. I have a burner phone that the bureau provided me with, and Savannah has direct orders not to use that phone number. Contact between us is kept to a minimum.

"Hot, right?" Hannah says with a wicked grin. "I hope he ends up as one of my patients today. I'd love to do a full physical exam on him."

"I never took you for the tattooed, bad boy type," I say. She's got a boyfriend at home. He's sweet, charming, and an accountant. There's not much of a fantasy wrapped up in that package.

Hannah is a ray of sunshine, and Mikhail is positively trouble. Thankfully, she's just looking and not going to ask for his phone number.

The elevator doors ding open. Hannah shuts her mouth, I do the same, and we step inside first.

Mikhail shuffles in as well, his suit coat off, draped over his arm. Accompanying him, is a bodyguard or one of his men. He has a half-dozen bodyguards based on the intel I reviewed before my undercover assignment.

I don't specifically recognize the gentleman, but Mikhail did a short stint in prison awaiting his trial. It's possible he made some new connections and grew his empire.

Neither appears to be injured or unwell at first glance. But Mikhail and his buddy could also be visiting a patient.

Or maybe he's making sure he didn't catch anything while behind bars. Who the hell knows why he's showing up today?

The man in the prestigious suit coat presses the button to the third floor. There are a wide array of physicians and medical offices on the third floor. It doesn't narrow down his reason for coming in today.

"Any lunch plans?" Hannah asks me, her mood downright chipper. Although she's talking to me, she's ogling the bratva leader. I'm confident that she has no idea who he is, or if she did, she'd shut it down right now.

"Just grabbing sandwiches with my new bestie?" I say, nudging her shoulder. "Assuming that we can get away for an hour."

Hannah chuckles. "You're lucky if you get a fifteen-minute break."

My first assignment is to connect with Mikhail without appearing like I genuinely want to. If he senses that I'm desperate, he'll see right through the charade. It must seem genuine, which is why he'll need to make the first move.

That's a tough sell in the elevator when he doesn't know anything about me.

But he's seen me.

That's the first step.

And now that he'll recognize me, hopefully, I can earn his trust.

The elevator dings, and Mikhail steps out along with his muscle, pretending that he didn't even notice us or acknowledge our existence.

Except he did notice me.

His gaze locks with mine downstairs, and while I have to pretend it's all business, there is something there. A spark that shouldn't have been, and a stirring of feelings that make my stomach flutter and my heart rate quicken.

After the double doors shut, I shoot a look at Hannah. I can't tell her he's bratva, but he gives off the bad boy vibe. "You and bad boys with tattoos?" I joke.

"My parents sent me to boarding school. I guess I'm still rebelling."

"Well, you'd better get it out of your system. Any day now, Mark is going to propose."

———

I've never been deep undercover. I did a week-long stint with the Sanchez Cartel eighteen months ago, but I didn't come anywhere close to their leader, and that's nothing compared to the viciousness of the bratva.

After work, I catch a glimpse of Agent Blakely outside. Savannah is keeping a low profile, but the moment I lock eyes with her, she gives me the signal for the second stage of our plan.

While I've been working diligently at the medical center as a nurse, the team back at the New York City field office has been digging up information on the bratva and gathering up intelligence to analyze.

I head down the block to grab my car, destined to break down on my way home. The vehicle will overheat, and the engine will die a few blocks from the bratva's compound if I'm lucky.

They had to pick the crappiest, coldest, and rainiest day in existence.

Some days, my job sucks.

I pull out of the parking garage and head down the block. Traffic is heavy, which isn't uncommon for

New York. If I weren't undercover, I'd ordinarily take the subway to the FBI field office from my house.

But as Madisyn Taylor, I drive to work daily in a used car that the agency purchased. Surprisingly, the vehicle still has four wheels attached, but it's well over two hundred thousand miles, and the outer body is an eyesore with its rust and paint discoloration.

Are nurses at the concierge center not paid well? It looks like I'm living paycheck to paycheck.

Is that the impression they want Mikhail to have? That I'm destitute and for him to take pity on me.

I have memorized the directions to the bratva compound, and the rental property that I'm staying in is located a few miles past the location.

Rain pelts the windshield, and I pop on the wipers, struggling to see through the onset of weather. I'm not looking forward to what comes next.

I'm a bundle of anxious energy, which I have to contain if I want this to go without a hitch. I've trained for this moment, going undercover, being able to rattle off a lie without being caught.

Heading down the road and away from the city's dense traffic, my check engine light pops on. I hit the gas a little harder, hoping that I'll be able to make it to my destination before the deluge outside drowns me.

The engine sputters, and the oil light pops on next. The FBI really wanted to make sure my car broke down. The engine produces a horrible clicking sound and dies just as I pull up within walking distance of the compound's fence.

I'd have preferred to be a bit closer. There are other nearby houses, but they're not the intended target.

I step out of the vehicle into the storm. It takes seconds for me to become soaked. I'm dripping wet, shivering, and my clothes are clinging to my skin.

I hustle toward the guard gate.

"Excuse me," I say. My teeth are chattering, and I'm not sure they can even understand the words coming from my mouth.

The guard pushes the window in his booth aside, sliding it to answer me. He's out of the rain, dry as a bone. "This is private property," he says. His voice is gruff, and he's got a thick Russian accent.

"My car broke down," I say and point at the vehicle a few yards away. I'm not sure if he can see it or not from his position inside of the booth, but he doesn't look the least bit concerned about helping me.

"Try your cell phone."

"It's dead." I pull my phone from my pocket. It's an older cell phone that the agency provided me with, a previous model that doesn't appear to give the same resemblance as a burner phone. The last thing I want is to draw more suspicion toward me.

If the battery hadn't been entirely drained earlier, then the deluge indeed killed my phone. I show it to the guard on duty.

He grumbles and picks up the landline phone. "I'll call a tow truck for you," he grunts.

As I stand out in the cold, shivering, soaking wet, with the rain continuing to pour, a black SUV with tinted windows pulls up to the gate.

The driver's window rolls down, and I recognize the man from earlier at the hospital, the bodyguard. Mikhail Barinov is seated in the front passenger seat.

The bodyguard doesn't say a word. He doesn't have to. My presence is enough to warrant an explanation.

"The girl says her car broke down," the gentleman in the booth answers. He opens the gate for their vehicle.

Thunder bellows out overhead.

Mikhail steps out into the deluge with an umbrella and hurries around to the passenger side to open the door for me. He slips out of his black wool coat, which is mostly dry, and drapes it over my shoulders. It's a warm and welcome relief from the cold clothes that cling to my skin.

"Come inside, dry off, and we'll get you on your way," he says and opens the back door.

I am shivering and trembling from the frigid weather. The coat keeps me from making a mess of the leather interior with my wet clothes. "Thanks," I say, and Mikhail shuts the door before stepping around to the passenger side.

The engine purrs as the driver hits the gas and guides the SUV forward past the open gates.

Shivering, I shove my arms into the warm coat and my hands into the pockets to get warm. My fingers graze over a small metallic rectangular object, a flash drive.

One-click Brutal Boss now!

ABOUT THE AUTHOR

Willow Fox has loved writing since she was in high school (many ages ago). Her small town romances are reflective of living in a small town in rural America.

Whether she's writing romance or sitting outside by the bonfire reading a good book, Willow loves the magic of the written word.

She dreams of being swept off her feet and hopes to do that to her readers!

Visit her website at:

https://authorwillowfox.com

ALSO BY WILLOW FOX

Eagle Tactical Series

Expose: Jaxson

Stealth: Mason

Conceal: Lincoln

Covert: Jayden

Truce: Declan

Mafia Marriages

Secret Vow

Captive Vow

Savage Vow

Unwilling Vow

Ruthless Vow

Bratva Brothers

Brutal Boss

Wicked Boss

Possessive Boss

Obsessive Boss

Dangerous Boss

Bossy Single Dad Series

Billionaire Grump

Mountain Grump

Bachelor Grump

Looking for kinkier books? Try these spicy stories written under the name Allison West.

Boxsets

Academy of Littles

Western Daddies Collection

Obey Daddy Collection

The Alpha Collection

Western Daddies

Her Billionaire Daddy

Her Cowboy Daddy

Her Outlaw Daddy

Her Forbidden Daddy

Standalone Romances

The Victorian Shift

Jailed Little Jade

Prefer a sweeter romance with action and adventure?
Check out these titles under the name Ruth Silver.

Aberrant Series

Love Forbidden

Secrets Forbidden

Magic Forbidden

Escape Forbidden

Refuge Forbidden

Boxsets

Gem Apocalypse

Nightblood

Royal Reaper

Royal Deception

Standalones

Stolen Art

www.ingramcontent.com/pod-product-compliance
Lightning Source LLC
Chambersburg PA
CBHW021036030726
47496CB00006B/1569